Contents

Into the Amazon

Chapter 1

The airplane shuddered, sending a splash of water from my plastic cup onto my tray table. I pulled my seat belt a little tighter across my lap and listened as the pilot came onto the intercom and announced that we were experiencing a little turbulence. He assured us that we would begin our descent into Manaus shortly.

My brother stirred awake and yawned. "Are we there yet?" he asked.

"Soon, Zac," I said. I wiped up the water with my napkin and returned to reading my grandmother's travel journal.

"What's Ama up to now?" he asked, leaning over to take a peek.

"She's hiking through the woods in Alaska," I told him.

I loved reading about Ama's travel adventures. It made me feel like I was along for the ride, like it was just the two of us together again—even though she passed away last year. She had been all over the world, and now here I was, exploring Brazil on my first international trip, far away from my hometown of St. Louis, Missouri.

"I'm on my way to the Amazon, Ama," I whispered, knowing how excited she would have been for me.

"Did you say something, Lea?" Zac asked. He leaned over me to look out the airplane window.

"Um, I said, 'I'm happy to be going to the rainforest with you.'"

"Ditto," he said. He stretched his arms out, and his elbow just missed my face.

"Watch it, Zac," I said, pushing his arm away.

"You'd better get used to close quarters," Zac said with a grin. "I mean, the Barros family's house is big enough, but it's no mansion. Don't worry, though—you're going to love my host family. Marcos is a tour guide and knows the Amazon rainforest better than anyone, and Olivia

is a second-grade teacher. And wait until you meet Tomás! He reminds me a lot of you when you were his age," Zac said.

I smiled, excited to be visiting the family Zac had been staying with during his college year abroad. We had spent the last week in a Brazilian beach town called Praia Tropical. I already missed the dazzling white beaches and the beautiful Atlantic Ocean—and I especially missed Camila, the new friend I had met there. After a week of getting to know each other and snorkeling and exploring together, it had been hard to say good-bye. I touched the wish bracelet she had given me. Its bright pink color symbol-ized friendship. I wished that our friendship would last forever.

I took out my camera. "Want to see my pho-tos of Praia Tropical?" I asked Zac.

"Are there any of Paloma and me?" he asked.

I smiled and handed over my camera.

Zac skimmed over my photos of colorful tide pools and Mom surfing the turquoise waves. Then he stopped at a photo of a girl his age with wavy black hair and a big smile. She was posing next to her beach shack. Paloma is my friend Camila's cousin, and she had taught me how to snorkel. Zac had a huge crush on her, and I couldn't help giggling as he stared wistfully at the photo.

Zac blushed and continued scrolling through the photos, pausing at a particularly dramatic image of Dad's helicopter rescue. We had gotten lost hiking when my father slipped and tumbled down the side of a cliff. He landed on a rocky platform just out of our reach. It was the scariest moment of my life, but Ama's compass inspired me to create a compass of my own—using my camera! Though it seemed like we were hopelessly lost, I was able to look at the photos I had taken during our hike and use the landmarks in the pictures to find our way back to town to get help.

I may have saved the day, but I couldn't save my father from ending up in a full leg cast. So much for his dream of hiking though the Amazon rainforest! Dad and Mom had agreed to let me go

to the rainforest with Zac, but decided it would be wisest for them to stay in Praia Tropical.

Out of habit, I reached for Ama's compass, which I usually kept on a chain around my neck. It had been very special to her, and she had given it to me shortly before she passed away. I had worn it every day until just yesterday, when I surrendered it to the ocean in honor of my grandmother during the Queen of the Sea celebration. When I put my hand where the necklace had been, I felt a flood of warmth wrap around me. Because no matter where I was or what I was doing, Ama would always be with me in my heart.

I reopened my grandmother's travel journal, eager to find out what amazing adventures she had experienced in Alaska.

I had no idea that a moose could be over seven feet tall! In a panic, I froze. It could have been the death of me. There he was, staring straight down at me—and there I was, all of five feet four inches. I slowly backed away to show him that I meant no harm. The moose either

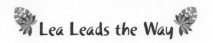
*got bored with me or realized that a visitor from
St. Louis wasn't much of a threat—because for
whatever reason, as I backed away, he turned
around and silently disappeared into the woods.*

Wow, I thought. *That was a close one.* I wondered what kinds of animals I'd encounter in the
Amazon rainforest.

The sound of light snoring made me turn to
Zac. He had fallen asleep with my camera in his
hands. A photo of Paloma and Zac wearing snorkeling gear was on the display. He was probably
dreaming about her.

I gently took the camera and scrolled
through the rest of the photos. The shimmer-
ing blue water and the sugary white sand were
beautiful, but what really took my breath away
were the underwater shots of coral reefs, colorful
sea life, and an old shipwreck on the ocean floor.
I paused at my favorite photo: dozens of baby
turtles hatching from their shells in the sand
and waddling toward the sea.

My best friend, Abby, and a lot of my other

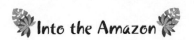

fifth-grade classmates had written comments on
my blog, saying that the turtle photo was their
favorite shot, too. *This is just the beginning,* I had
written back. *Just wait until you see the pictures I
plan to take in the Amazon rainforest. I'm going to post
lots of photos of exotic jungle animals!*

    I couldn't wait for my next adventure to
begin.

Bem-Vinda!

Chapter 2

When Zac told me that Manaus was in the middle of the rainforest, I had imagined that we'd land in a clearing in the jungle. So picture my surprise when the plane broke through the clouds and I saw a city skyline. Manaus looked as big as St. Louis—maybe even bigger! I never would have guessed that there was a huge city in the middle of the Amazon rainforest.

After Zac and I gathered our bags, we waited on the curb outside the airport for our ride. Soon, a man in a battered green truck drove up and leapt out. By the way he and Zac greeted each other with wide smiles and a big hug, I knew the man must be Marcos Barros.

"Lea! *Bem-vinda!* Welcome to Manaus!" I instantly felt at home with Marcos as he headed

toward me with his arms open. His tanned face was friendly and his brown eyes sparkled like he was ready to laugh. Marcos's black hair was pulled back in a ponytail, and he wore a chocolate-brown seed necklace around his neck.

"That's a beautiful necklace," I told him. "Did you make it yourself?"

He touched the beads at his throat. "This was a gift from an indigenous rainforest tribe." His eyes brightened as he reached around his neck to unclasp it. "I want you to have it."

"Oh, no!" I protested. "I couldn't. It's yours!"

"A gift from me to you," Marcos said. "Please, I insist. It would make me happy."

Zac laughed. "Marcos is very persuasive," he said. "You may as well just take it now. Otherwise, you'll argue for hours—and end up with it anyway!"

"Thank you. *Obrigada*," I said, blushing as Zac helped me put on the necklace. I liked the feel of the beads around my neck. They were the size of small marbles, and were smooth and soothing to the touch.

I climbed into the backseat and buckled my seat belt as Marcos loaded our suitcases into the back of the truck. I was eager to get on the road and head to the rainforest as soon as possible so that I could see some exotic animals. I wondered which animals I'd encounter first: maybe a jaguar or a caiman, and of course, monkeys. There were certain to be monkeys!

Abby had made me promise to take plenty of photos. She loves animals, just like me. Her mom is a veterinarian, and they have lots of pets and foster animals. One time, they fostered a miniature potbellied pig. He was so cute!

I gazed out the window as we left the airport and headed toward downtown Manaus. "Um, excuse me, Marcos, but how far is the rainforest from here?" I asked.

"It's almost four hours to Santa Sofia," Marcos replied.

Four hours! I wasn't sure I could wait that long. But before I could worry about it, we passed by a beautiful building that took my breath away. Huge and majestic, it was painted

pink with white pillars and had sweeping steps like something out of a fairy tale.

"Wow," I said, pressing my hands against the window.

"That's the Amazon Theater opera house. It's one hundred and twenty years old," Marcos said, pulling over the truck so I could get a better look.

I wished my parents were here. Dad's a history professor and Mom's an architect who restores historic buildings. I took out my camera, knowing they'd want to see this.

"I didn't expect something like this in the middle of the rainforest," I said as I focused my camera on the green-and-yellow tiled dome at the top of the grand theater.

"There's lots of culture and art in Manaus," Marcos explained. "It is the biggest city in the Amazon rainforest. Over two million people live here."

Zac turned to me. "That's more than six times the population of St. Louis!"

I raised my eyebrows in surprise.

Marcos grinned and pulled back onto the

road. "Before we start the long drive to Santa Sofia, I've got someplace special to show you," he said, glancing at me in the rearview mirror. "It's one of my favorite places to take visitors. They just love it."

"The coffee?" Zac asked. His eyes sparkled with amusement.

Marcos nodded and laughed. "Yes, the coffee. I know how much you love the coffee."

I smiled awkwardly. Coffee? We were going to get coffee? Coffee is so gross—and sneaky, too! It smells delicious, but once I snuck a taste of my dad's and it was so bitter that I spit it out. Didn't Zac know I wasn't old enough to drink coffee? Over the past week of our trip, I had been trying very hard to remind my brother that I wasn't his baby sister anymore. Maybe I had overdone it!

Zac saw the look on my face and laughed. "Don't worry, Lea. We won't make you drink the coffee."

I was still wondering about their inside joke when Marcos parked the truck near the river. Automatically, I grabbed my camera, and was

glad that I had. Everywhere I looked was a photo
waiting to happen. Huge, fresh-caught fish lay on
beds of ice, and the smell was, well … fishy! By
the time we got to the dock, I had grown used to
the smell, but I was still a little freaked out by all
the fish lying there and staring at me.

"*Oi!*" Marcos called to a man in a small
speedboat. The man greeted him and waved for
us to join him.

"Hop in. This is for us!" Zac declared.

I looked at Zac, confused, and carefully
climbed into the boat. We were going on a boat to
get coffee? The river was huge and the opposite
shore seemed miles away. Surely Zac and Marcos
could find coffee on this side of the river.

Zac's eyes lit up as he secured my life jacket.
"Hold on to your camera, Lea," he said. "We're
going to go fast."

"Okay," I said. My confusion quickly turned
into excitement. Speeding on the river to a myste-
rious destination? I was up for that!

We pushed back from the dock and motored
slowly to the middle of the river. Then we took off.

The wind whipped through my hair as I watched the shore and the city get farther and farther away, and then *vrooom!* Suddenly we were cutting through the water so fast that I had to grip Zac's arm for support.

"Yippee!" he yelled like a cowboy, waving to the bigger tourist boats as we sped past.

"Look!" Marcos yelled over the roar of the boat's engine. He pointed straight ahead.

I peered over the bow of the boat. Ahead of us, it looked like the river was split in two: The left half was dark black and the right half was creamy brown. I couldn't believe my eyes!

As the speedboat slowed to a stop, Marcos explained, "This is where the Rio Negro and the Solimões River converge. It's called the Meeting of the Waters."

"Like Mom and Dad's coffee," Zac said, sweeping his arm across the scene like a model showing off the prizes on a game show.

I laughed. *Now* I understood. My father always insists on strong, black coffee. But Mom adds so much cream to her mug that Dad always

14

jokes, "Would you like some coffee with your cream?"

"How far do the rivers stay separate like this?" I asked Marcos.

"For miles," he said. "But eventually, the rivers merge and blend." He reached over the side of the boat and swirled his hand in the water. "Go ahead," he urged. "Feel the water."

Cautiously, I dipped my hand into the water and moved it around. I could totally feel the difference. The black water was cold and the brown water was warm.

I broke into a grin. "This is so weird—I love it!"

I sat back and started taking photos and a short video for my blog. What a great way to start my Amazon adventure!

A Surprise Snack

Chapter 3

I couldn't wait to get to the rainforest. Marcos put the truck in gear, and as we began our four-hour journey, I had my camera ready. I was tired and wished I had slept more on the plane, like Zac, but now I was too excited to sleep. After all, I hadn't traveled halfway around the world to take a nap! I wanted to see the animals—wild, exotic animals!—and I wasn't about to let anything stop me. But before I knew it, the hum of the truck's engine and the warm breeze from the open window began to lull me to sleep. I fought to keep my eyes open, determined not to miss anything.

I awoke with a start and rubbed my eyes. How long had I been asleep? On both sides of the truck, thick bushes and trees brushed past. It looked like I was in another world. I sat straight

up when it hit me. The rainforest! We were driving through the thick of the rainforest.

"Why didn't you wake me?" I asked Zac.

"You needed to sleep, Lea," he said, turning to look at me. "You're here for a week. You've got plenty of time to see the rainforest."

But I didn't want to waste one minute. I held my camera up, ready for my first photo of a wild animal. I hoped it would be a jaguar. I craned my neck, eager to take in my surroundings. Even though it was early February, everything was so lush and green here—unlike back home in St. Louis, where the tree branches were bare and snow blanketed the ground.

The bumpy dirt road had very little traffic. After forty-five minutes, we had passed one car with music blasting out of its open windows, a van with a mattress strapped to the top of it, and a teenage girl riding a brown horse. I took her photo for my blog. But aside from the horse, I didn't see a single animal—not even a bird!

My stomach rumbled louder than the truck's engine.

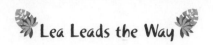

"Hungry?" Marcos asked.

"Maybe a little," I admitted sheepishly.

"A little?" Zac joked. "That growl was so loud, I'm sure Mom and Dad could hear it all the way in Praia Tropical!"

I ignored him.

"Olivia is preparing a meal for us at home," Marcos said, "but we can stop for a snack."

I wondered where we'd go. There certainly weren't any restaurants or fast-food places that I could see. Marcos pulled the truck over next to a group of palm trees and we all got out. It felt good to stretch my legs. There was a cooler in the back of the truck, and Marcos pulled out a bottle of papaya juice for each of us.

"How about some really fresh food?" Marcos asked. It looked like he was suppressing a smile.

I looked around for a mango tree, or maybe we'd have those little bananas that I'd enjoyed in Praia Tropical. Instead, Marcos built a circle of small rocks and gathered some dry moss to place in the center. Then he picked some small brown nuts off a nearby tree and laid them on a huge,

waxy leaf that was wider and longer than a football. He reached into his pocket and took out a stone. I watched as he struck his knife against it with lightning precision, starting a fire in the moss.

Roasted nuts! I thought to myself. This would be a treat. During the winter holidays in St. Louis, we sometimes had roasted chestnuts. I wondered if these would taste the same.

Ama had written in her travel journal that she always enjoyed trying the local dishes of each place she visited. *It's my chance to try something different,* she wrote, *and maybe even discover a new favorite food!* Over the past week in Praia Tropical, I had tasted a delicious seafood stew called *moqueca*, lots of scrumptious pastries, and exotic fruits I'd never seen before—and loved them. Maybe whatever Marcos had in store would be my new favorite!

Marcos sliced open the nuts and laid them face-up on the leaf over the fire. Something was squirming inside! I made a face and waited for him to notice that these nuts were bad. Clearly,

he'd have to go back and pick new nuts—ones
that didn't have worms in them.

I looked on, horrified, as Marcos scooped the
fat, white, wormy-looking things from the nut-
shells and skewered them on a stick.

"Wh-what are those?" I asked, my voice
cracking with disbelief.

"They're grubs," Zac said matter-of-factly.
"You know, larvae. Baby insects."

"You don't expect me to eat live worms, do
you?" I asked, taking a step back.

Marcos laughed and shook his head. "Of
course not—I'm going to cook them first." Then
he did the unthinkable—he roasted them over the
flames.

After about a minute, he inspected the grubs
and pulled one off the skewer. "Here, Lea," he
said, offering one to me. "It's *saboroso*—very tasty!
Enjoy it while it's hot!"

My eyes grew big. There was no way I was
going to eat a worm!

"Go ahead, Lea," Zac goaded me. "Eat it.
You're not scared, are you?"

A Surprise Snack

I bristled. I'd show Zac that I wasn't afraid! In Praia Tropical I had promised myself that I wouldn't be scared to test myself and try new things. That was something I had learned from Ama.

I couldn't let my fears stop me now.

Marcos and Zac were waiting for me.

My throat constricted as I took a grub from Marcos, who was munching on a handful of them. The plump white larva had turned toasty brown over the fire, and it was still hot. I took a deep breath. Determined, I stared straight at Zac, popped the grub into my mouth, shut my eyes, and chewed.

Don't spit it out, don't spit it out, I said to myself. *Don't. Spit. It. Out.*

It was nutty and meaty and *almost* tasty—but I was still totally grossed out. I tried not to gag.

Finally, I swallowed the grub and looked triumphantly at Zac. "Okay, your turn," I dared him. I reached for my papaya juice and finished the bottle.

"Are you kidding?" my brother said.

"There's no way I'd eat one of those! Lea, you're either really crazy or really brave."

Marcos grinned. "I'd say she's really brave," he said. "Even braver than you, Zac!"

"You're right," my brother said, giving me a wink.

"Here, Lea." Marcos offered me the stick with a couple of roasted grubs on it. "You want to finish these?"

"Um, no thanks, I'm full," I said. I still couldn't believe what I had just done.

I took out my camera and photographed the remaining grubs. This would really shock my classmates! As gross as it was, I couldn't wait to blog about it. One kid from my class, Dax, used to tease me and call me a scaredy-cat—all because when we went on a field trip to a dairy farm in third grade, I had been afraid to milk a cow. I'd like to see him call me a scaredy-cat now!

Meet the Family

Chapter 4

After another hour of driving, we veered off the dirt road and onto a paved, double-lane street. Zac let me know that we weren't far from the Barros family's home. Santa Sofia, he told me, was the last town accessible by road in this area of the rainforest.

As we paused at a stoplight, I recognized the lively main street from photos that my brother had e-mailed to us when he first arrived. A grocer was piling watermelons into a wooden cart, shopkeepers motioned customers inside their stores as music blasted onto the streets, and shaded restaurant patios were packed with diners. Every now and then, Marcos honked his horn and someone would wave to us.

We turned down a bumpy road that ran

along the river, passing colorful houses set near
the water's edge. Some were on stilts, while others
actually floated on the water. At last, the truck
ground to a stop in front of a stilted wooden
house painted a cheerful yellow. Chickens milled
about in the huge yard, and the trees were dotted
with fragrant white flowers. I glimpsed a trio of
toucans perched on a branch and snapped their
photo. Finally, some real wildlife!

A tall woman with a friendly smile raced
outside to meet us. She was wearing her hair in
twin braids. I admired her colorful cotton dress.
It reminded me of the one Camila had given me
when we said good-bye.

The woman hugged Zac, and then turned to
me. "Lea," she said, giving me a warm embrace.
"I am Olivia, Zac's host mother. Zac has told us so
many wonderful things about you!"

I blushed and said, *"Muito prazer,"* which Zac
had taught me to say when I met someone new. I
glanced toward the house just in time to see the
rose-colored curtains stir and move slightly to the
side. Someone—or something—was watching us.

Olivia turned to see what I was looking at and shook her head. "Tomás, *vem!* Come! Zac is home."

The front door opened slowly. A small boy around five years old raced out and hid behind Olivia's legs. From what I could see, he had dark black hair like his father, and his complexion was lighter like his mother's. He peeked out at me with big curious brown eyes and long eyelashes, and then ran and hid behind Marcos. Moments later, he made a break for it and raced into my brother's arms. In one fluid motion, Zac picked him up and twirled him around, just like he used to do with me when I was little. The boy squealed with delight and buried his face in Zac's shoulder.

"Lea, there's someone special I want you to meet," Zac said, grinning widely. "This young fellow here is Tomás! Tomás, *esta é a minha irmã*—this is my sister, Lea."

Tomás clung to Zac the way he had to his mother. Every now and then, he peered out to look at me. Each time I waved, he'd hide again. I continued playing peekaboo with Tomás until

I felt something nipping my shoe. I looked down to see a colorful red-and-orange rooster pecking at my shoelaces.

Startled, I yelped and jumped away. When I ran, the rooster chased me. Finally, I leapt onto a tree stump at the edge of the yard. The rooster growled and strutted around me.

"What happened to the big brave Lea?" Zac teased.

"Galo Louco!" Marcos yelled at the chicken. He turned to Tomás and gestured at him to help me.

Tomás ran toward me and scooped up the rooster. Then he set him down in a small fenced-off area of the yard near a red wooden henhouse.

"Please excuse Galo Louco. He's our crazy rooster," Olivia said apologetically as she helped me down off the tree stump. "Not too friendly, but he watches out for our chickens, and they lay the best eggs. This yard is his roost, and he's jealous of you!"

Hmm. I wasn't sure whether to feel honored or nervous that a crazy chicken was jealous of me.

I made a mental note to try to avoid any future encounters with Galo Louco.

When Marcos had said that Olivia was preparing a meal for us, he had neglected to tell me that it was more like a feast. Thick slices of fresh watermelon, mango, and pineapple were piled high on a platter alongside fruits I'd never heard of, such as *carambola*, a sour fruit shaped like a star, and jackfruit, which reminded me of a tart banana. Next to that were plates of grilled fish, corn cakes, and cheesy rolls called *pão de queijo*.

We sat on long benches on either side of the table. Olivia made sure that my plate was never empty. I especially liked the tapioca pancakes stuffed with bananas.

"Try the goat cheese," Olivia said, passing me the plate. "Our neighbors down the river raise goats, and this was made from their milk," she said.

Fresh goat cheese and grubs in one day! Now *that* was something blog-worthy.

As we feasted, I told Olivia and Marcos about the blog I was writing about my trip in Brazil. "My classmates can't wait to hear about the rainforest," I said.

Olivia told me that all her students had been very excited when Zac visited her class to talk about his rainforest studies. "But I think they were most excited to hear about how different life is in St. Louis. They thought it was funny that students in the United States take a bus to school instead of riding a boat!"

"A school boat?" I asked, tickled by the thought of it.

Olivia nodded as she cut up a piece of fish on Tomás's plate. "Tomás just completed kindergarten, and in two years he'll be in my class."

I looked at Tomás, who peered at me nervously and scooted closer to Zac. I could tell that he still wasn't too sure about me. And could I blame him? I had to admit that I hadn't made a good first impression by running around the yard in fear of a chicken.

As the conversation continued, I couldn't help

noticing Tomás and Zac. They whispered with their heads close together, and Zac kept making Tomás laugh by making funny faces. I felt a tug on my heart, remembering that Zac used to do that with me when I was little.

"What do you think, Lea?" Marcos said as he handed me the platter of tropical fruit. "It would be a great story for your blog."

I blushed. "Excuse me, I spaced out for a second. What did you ask me?"

"I was asking if I could take you and Zac out on the river in the morning," Marcos repeated.

"Oh, yes!" I said a little too loudly. Trying to be more subdued, I added, "That would be nice, thank you."

As much as I was enjoying dinner, I couldn't wait until tomorrow morning, when I'd be sailing down the famed Amazon River, exploring the rainforest, and seeing wild animals up close at last!

Once we had finished dinner and cleaned up, Olivia helped me get settled in Tomás's room. It looked a lot like Abby's little brother's room. Lots of books lined the bookshelves, posters of soccer players decorated the walls, and crayon drawings of rainforest animals were pinned on a bulletin board. On the bed was a pile of stuffed animals, and I noticed one well-worn, goofy-looking monkey that seemed to be the most loved.

"I can sleep on the couch," I told Olivia as she put fresh sheets on the bed.

"It's fine," she assured me. "You'll be more comfortable here. Tomás will sleep with us."

The little boy peered at me from behind his mother. His bangs almost touched his eyelashes. Olivia said something to him in Portuguese and he nodded solemnly.

"Bath time," Olivia explained to me. "He hates the idea of taking a bath—but once he's in the tub, it's impossible to get him out!"

After a few minutes, I could hear Tomás singing and splashing around. I sat down at his small desk with my tablet. Even though I was exhausted, I was determined to post a blog about my first day

in the Amazon rainforest. I included photos of the grubs, and typed a caption:

> It's not quite as good as St. Louis's famous gooey butter cake, but this local treat tastes nutty, probably because the larvae—a.k.a. grubs—were nestled in the center of palm nuts. Roasted, they don't taste half bad! Who knows what else I'll see—and eat—tomorrow!

After I posted to my blog, I checked my e-mail. There was one from Mom and Dad asking if we had made it safely. This was my first trip apart from them.

Camila had written to me saying she missed me already. I looked at my pink wish bracelet. I had wished that Camila and I would stay friends forever; the legend was that my wish would come true when the bracelet fell off on its own. I wrote back to tell her I missed her too. *P.S. I'm keeping my fingers crossed that you'll be able to visit St. Louis soon!* I added.

Tomás came back into his room, freshly

scrubbed and in his pajamas. Without taking his eyes off me, he gathered some books and picked up his stuffed monkey.

"*Macaco,*" Tomás said, holding up the monkey. Then he pointed to himself. "*Meu macaco!*"

I nodded. "Your monkey," I said. "Thank you for lending me your room, Tomás. Obrigada."

He backed out the door. Then he held up Macaco again and said, "Meu!" before turning around and running down the hall.

I tried not to laugh. When I was little, I had a stuffed animal that Ama had brought back for me from Thailand. I named her Ellie the Elephant. Ellie meant the world to me, so I knew how Tomás felt. I still keep Ellie on my desk in my room.

I turned off my tablet and crawled into bed. Just as I was about to lie down, Tomás raced back into the room, grabbed the pillow out from under me, and disappeared.

I hit my head on the headboard, but shook it off and reached for the other pillow. I was exhausted. Not long ago, I had listened to the

rhythmic music of the ocean's waves as I drifted off to sleep. Tonight I was serenaded by the quiet of the rainforest, the rustle of the leaves in the breeze, and the murmur of Portuguese as Olivia and Marcos spoke softly to each other in the next room.

Feeling relaxed, I opened Ama's travel journal and began to read. But I only got a few paragraphs in before I fell asleep.

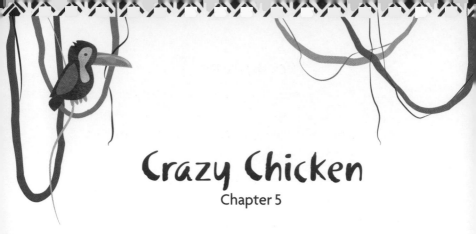

Crazy Chicken
Chapter 5

It seemed like I had just closed my eyes when I awoke to the sounds of Zac and Marcos talking and pans clattering. I quickly got dressed, excited to start my first day of exploring the rainforest.

"Bom dia!" Marcos said brightly when I wandered into the kitchen. He was slicing a fresh, juicy pineapple into chunks. Tomás stood on a stool at the counter, carefully placing bread on a plate one slice at a time and making sure it was stacked evenly.

"Bom dia," I responded, rubbing my eyes. I glanced at the clock. 5:00? What!? What was I doing up at five o'clock on my vacation? I yawned. "Why is everybody up so early?" I asked.

"Because Marcos has to give morning tours before it gets too hot outside," Zac shouted over

the whirr of the coffee grinder. "And he promised to take us on our tour first."

"Lea, would you mind gathering some eggs from the henhouse for our breakfast?" Olivia asked. She was stirring a pot full of beans on the stove. "Seven or eight should be fine."

I stepped outside and looked for Galo Louco. *Phew,* I thought. *The coast is clear.* The gate was open and a few of the chickens were outside pecking at the ground. Some were brown, others were reddish, and still others were a combination of both colors. I picked up a worn woven basket near the gate and hooked it over the crook of my arm. I walked up the ramp to the henhouse and ducked through the short doorway.

Inside, about a dozen hens sat on their eggs, making low, soothing clucking noises. They didn't seem very interested in me. The first couple of eggs were easy to gather from the unoccupied beds. *This is sort of fun,* I thought. I felt like a farmer. I made a mental note to return later to take pictures for my blog.

As I continued gathering the eggs, I heard a

growling sound. I looked down, and facing me was none other than Galo Louco. I averted my eyes and continued gathering eggs. *Three, four, five . . .*

Suddenly Galo Louco began squawking and pecking at my sandals.

"Shoo! Shoo!" I shouted. Then he squawked louder and started chasing me around the small henhouse. I screamed, dropped the basket, and ran, hitting my head on the doorway on the way out.

When I rushed back into the Barroses' house and told Olivia what had happened, Zac rolled his eyes. "It does no good if you gather eggs but leave them in the henhouse," he told me.

I forced a laugh, but I was embarrassed. It was bad enough that Olivia had to put ice on my forehead where I had hit it, but when she sent little Tomás back to get the eggs, I felt like an idiot.

I quickly forgot my embarrassment when I started eating breakfast. I had never had eggs as fresh or delicious as the ones Olivia fried up.

"Zac," I asked as I reached for seconds, "after

Marcos takes us on the river tour this morning, can we go on a hike?"

Zac sopped up some beans with his bread and shoveled it into his mouth. "I'm not sure you're ready," he said.

"Ready? Of course I'm ready!" I said confidently.

"But if you're scared of a little chicken, what will you do if you see an anaconda?" Zac said with his mouth full.

I rolled my eyes. "I've held lots of snakes at the St. Louis Zoo," I reminded him.

"True," Zac mused. "You're the only little kid who ever volunteered. But an Amazon anaconda is one of the biggest snakes in the world. They can grow as long as a bus and weigh over 500 pounds!" His eyes lit up. My brother had always loved snakes. When he was in high school, Zac had an impressive collection of lifelike rubber snakes, and we often heard screams in the house whenever Dad or Mom found one hidden in the towels or under the sheets.

Marcos took a sip of coffee. "Anacondas

squeeze their prey to death," he said casually. "But you probably don't need to worry about one chasing you down. In fact, the most dangerous animal in the jungle is not a big one, like the giant river otter, which can be up to six feet long. Nor the pirarucu fish, which grows up to nine feet long and over 200 pounds. No, the most dangerous animal in the Amazon is actually the tiny mosquito, because it can carry diseases."

I nodded. Now I was glad Mom had made me get shots before traveling, even though I wasn't thrilled at the time.

I looked Zac in the eye. "I'll be fine."

Zac shrugged and gave me a playful wink.

"We had better get going if we want to get a good boat ride in before my first tour," Marcos said. He started gathering the plates.

"You all go ahead," Olivia said. "Tomás and I will clean up."

After I slathered myself with enough sunscreen to create a solar eclipse, I reached for the

insect repellent. Zac did an exaggerated cough and waved at the air in front of him as I doused myself with so much bug spray that any insect unfortunate enough to land on me would just slide off.

"There aren't many mosquitos here on the water," Marcos explained as he lifted a tarp off his motorized canoe. The bright red boat was fairly big and could seat up to a dozen people. I noticed that Marcos had painted the name *Tomás* in swirly script on the boat's side.

"Oh, I thought this place would be full of mosquitos," I said. I stepped into the boat carefully and snapped the buckles on my life jacket.

"The acid in the water repels them," Marcos explained. "But if it's mosquitos you're interested in, I'm sure there will be plenty who'd love to meet you when you're hiking through the rainforest!"

I cringed and gave him a weak smile.

Rocky hills and walls of tall green trees and plants rose up on both sides of the river. It was already very hot even though the sun had only just begun to rise. But the wind felt nice as we sped along the river. I loved looking behind us as the canoe cut through the black-blue water, leaving a bubbly white trail in its wake.

Marcos slowed the boat as we entered what looked like a hidden tunnel of plants and branches. It was so beautiful I could hardly contain my excitement. Marcos cut the engine and unhooked the oars from the edge of the boat. I listened to the soft splashes of Marcos's paddle entering the water as he maneuvered the boat through a maze of tangled tree roots. Zac lifted a lantern so that we could see better. The black water reflected the plants and trees all around us, as if we were gliding over a mirror.

"See these plants?" Zac said, gesturing around us. "Those are actually treetops. The trunks are underwater. When the rainy season ends and the water level lowers, you could walk around the bottom of this river right here."

"The trees can live like that?" I asked. It was hard to imagine. But then I remembered the tide pools Zac had shown me in Praia Tropical. There, I had been able to walk on the coral and rock,

knowing that during high tide, it would all be under the sea.

"Where are all the animals?" I asked, motioning around me.

"Well, there are piranhas right below you," Zac said.

"Seriously?" I asked, instinctively tucking my feet up off the bottom of the canoe.

"Seriously," Marcos said. He pulled out a couple of bamboo fishing rods and handed them to me and Zac.

Zac pulled a small plastic bag out of his pocket. "Put this on the hook," my brother instructed, handing me a small chunk of meat.

I watched Zac bait his hook, and then I did the same.

Then we waited. And waited. Zac got a couple of bites, but when he tried to reel them in, the fish got away. All of a sudden there was a tug on my fishing pole.

"Yank it up!" Zac cried.

"Be careful," Marcos cautioned, as I stood up. "Yank fast, but in a small movement."

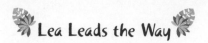

I wasn't about to let this fish go. I wanted to catch a fish before my brother did!

"I've got it. I'll be careful," I assured them ... right before I tripped over the cooler.

I accidentally threw my fishing pole up into the air as I splashed headfirst into the Amazon River—filled with man-eating piranhas!

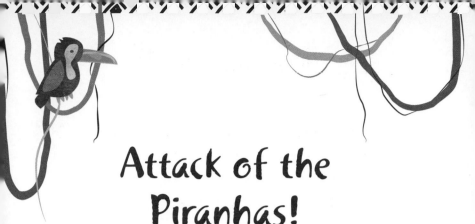

Attack of the
Piranhas!
Chapter 6

Panic washed over me. Flailing, I grasped for the edge of the canoe, kicking my legs to ward off any of the vicious piranhas that may have wanted to devour me.

What was that? I shuddered as something skimmed my leg. I screamed and kicked at something wrapped around my big toe.

As I gripped the canoe, I felt Zac's and Marcos's strong arms lifting me into the boat. "It's got me!" I yelled, pointing at my foot. I was afraid to look.

"You're fine!" Zac laughed, and I felt him pull something off my toe. "See?" He held up a clump of river weed.

Gasping, I managed to sputter "thank you" to Zac and Marcos as I tried to catch my breath.

"You okay?" Zac asked as he reached for my flip-flops floating on the river's surface. "I know how much you loved snorkeling, but isn't this a bit much?"

"How can you joke at a time like this?" I cried. "I could have been eaten alive!"

Marcos wrapped a towel around my shoulders. "I'm glad you're okay. But it's actually a myth that piranhas eat humans," he explained as he cast his own fishing line into the water. "In 1913, your president Theodore Roosevelt decided to tour the Amazon. So the local people came up with a plan to impress him. They caught piranhas, isolated them, and starved them. When Roosevelt arrived, the locals threw a live cow into the water and the piranhas devoured it. Roosevelt wrote about what he saw—and the myth that piranhas are ruthless killers was born."

"You're kidding," I said. So all this time the piranhas' reputation for being man-eaters was an urban legend—or rather, an Amazon legend!

"So much about the rainforest is misunderstood," Zac chimed in. "People want to believe that it's this untouchable place filled with deadly piranhas, and that there are so many trees that the forest is infinite."

I was about to ask Zac what he meant when Marcos tugged on his fishing pole. "Aha!" he yelled. "*This* is a piranha!" He held up a small, squirming fish. He removed it from his fishing hook and held its body with a firm grip so that it couldn't wriggle away. It was dark brown and flat, and I could see its tiny sharp teeth. "Watch," Marcos said. He held up a leaf to the piranha's mouth and it chomped away at it. "It might bite you, but it certainly isn't going to devour you. So the next time you fall into the water, Lea," he said with a wink, "just remember that you don't need to worry about the piranhas." He tossed the little piranha back into the water and turned to me. "It's the caimans, electric eels, and water snakes that you have to watch out for."

When he saw my eyes widen, Marcos added, "As long as you follow the safety rules and re-spect the wildlife, you'll be safe. Animals won't bite if you leave them alone."

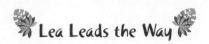

Zac nodded. "Believe me, Lea, the animals' idea of a good time is not to hang out and have humans for supper, but for us to leave them alone. By splashing around in the water like that, you disturbed their habitat."

I stared at him with my mouth hanging open in disbelief. Was he seriously taking the *piranhas'* side?

Marcos started paddling again, past the maze of roots and plants. We emerged from the curtain of leaves, and I shaded my eyes from the bright sunlight that was just beginning to peek over the trees. Once we reached the middle of the river, Marcos started the boat's engine and we zoomed ahead. The warm wind whipped through my still-damp hair like the best blow-dryer in the world. In the distance, I could see the Barroses' yellow house. It looked tiny, like a dollhouse. I was eager to get out of my wet clothes, but sorry that the river cruise was already over.

After I had showered and changed into fresh clothes, I went outside for some time alone. I scanned the yard for Galo Louco, and was glad

to see that he was penned up behind the fence.
I walked to the dock and waved to Marcos as
he motored away to pick up the first of his tour
groups. Then I sat on the edge of the dock for a
long time, thinking about how brave I had felt just
a few days ago in Praia Tropical. Now I felt like a
coward. I had been in the rainforest for less than
twenty-four hours and already the two kinds of
animals I had come into contact with had scared
me—and one was just a dumb chicken! What
would I do if I really did come face-to-face with
an anaconda—or a jaguar?

My thoughts were interrupted by the sound
of a screen door slamming shut. I looked up to
see Tomás bolt out of the house and scramble up
a massive, gnarled tree in the yard. Shortly after,
Zac came out.

"Tomás, *onde você está?*" he called out. Then
he noticed me on the dock. "Lea, have you seen
Tomás? We're playing hide-and-go-seek!"

"If I told you, wouldn't that be cheating?"
I asked, heading toward him. I glanced at the tree
and smiled. The leaves rustled, and I could see

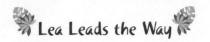
one of Tomás's legs among the branches.

Zac looked up. *"Está aí,* Tomás?" he asked. "Are you there?"

"Não estou aqui," Tomás replied.

Zac chuckled. "He says he isn't there."

I laughed along. When I was little, I used to love playing hide-and-go-seek with Zac. Now, here he was halfway across the world playing the same game with his new family.

"Tomás?" Zac called up.

In an instant, Tomás scrambled down the tree and leapt into Zac's arms, laughing. I felt a strange twinge watching the two of them. My brother seemed so comfortable here with Tomás and his host parents. He seemed like he was at home.

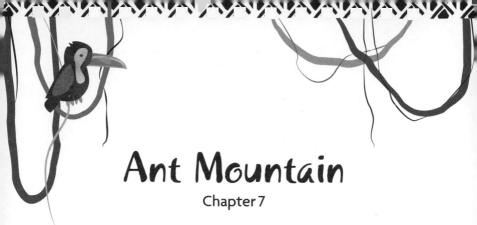

Ant Mountain

Chapter 7

After lunch, I opened up my tablet to read my classmates' comments on yesterday's blog post. The first comment was from Dax, the boy who always calls me a scaredy-cat.

> I don't believe you. Are you really in the rainforest? Where are all the wild animals?

That's what I wanted to know! I was determined not only to see some myself, but to photograph them and post the photos to my blog for my classmates to see. I responded with a short blog post about this morning's river cruise:

> The rainforest is unlike any place I have ever seen or even imagined. Even the air is different

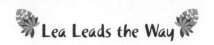

here—it's humid and smells like a greenhouse.
There are walls of plants that tower up and
block out the sun. And the Amazon River,
well . . . though it might not have been my plan
to go for a swim, I did! I fell in headfirst! I'm lucky
the piranhas didn't get me . . . or the caimans . . .
or the electric eels!

I smiled. *That should satisfy Dax,* I thought. *At
least for now.* I logged off and went into the living
room to remind Zac that he had said he'd take me
on a hike today.

Tomás wanted to join us, but Olivia made
him stay behind so that Zac and I could have
some time to ourselves. I was secretly glad that
he wasn't tagging along. Tomás was cute, but I
couldn't help feeling a little jealous whenever I
saw Zac playing with him like he used to do with
me. In fact, it seemed like Zac had forgotten that
he had a *real* sibling right here in Santa Sofia.

It was almost as if my brother was more
interested in being a part of the Barros family
than our own family. I wondered what my mom

and dad were doing. I'd had lots of sleepovers at Abby's, but I had never been this far away from my parents before. Being fifteen hundred miles apart was a lot different from being three blocks away, and e-mailing was not the same as being in the same room.

Zac had the rest of the year to be with Tomás, but only one week with me. It would be nice, I thought, to have my brother to myself for a while.

As we walked through the rainforest, I was on high alert any time I heard a sound, thinking it might be an animal nearby. I stopped so often that I almost lost sight of Zac a couple of times. *Yikes*, I thought. Getting lost in the rainforest was absolutely the last thing I wanted to do.

The rainforest was dense with tropical trees and plants. At times it was hard to see the dirt path that meandered in and out of hidden passages, through bushes, and under and over fallen tree branches. Zac had no problem climbing over the branches, but one was a struggle for me. I tripped

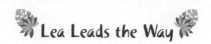

and scraped my knee and cried out with surprise.

Zac was by my side instantly. "You okay, Lea?" he asked.

"Yeah, I'm totally fine," I assured him. "Let's keep going!"

"Okay, but keep your voice down or else you'll scare away all the animals."

My eyes lit up, but I contained my excitement. Just to be sure that we couldn't get lost, I kept taking photos of landmarks in case we needed to backtrack, the way I had during our hike in Praia Tropical. I got so busy taking photos that I lost sight of Zac.

Instinctively, I reached for Ama's compass necklace, but instead I touched the seed necklace that Marcos had given me. I took a deep breath. *Don't panic*, I reminded myself. Zac couldn't be far away. I wanted to call for him, but I didn't want to ruin my chances of seeing the animals.

I cupped my hands. "Zac?" I called in a loud whisper. "Where are you?"

Something hit my shoulder. An anaconda? A giant spider? I flinched and spun around.

Zac was standing behind me. "Man, you're jumpy," he whispered. "What's the matter?"

"Um, nothing," I said, shaking off my nerves. *Come on, Lea,* I told myself. *Get it together.* "I was hoping that we'd see more wild animals," I said as I followed Zac through a dense wall of vines. "I mean, besides the piranhas we saw this morning."

"If you pay attention, you'll find that they're all around us," Zac said.

I raised my camera, but I didn't see any movement amidst the leaves. Zac must have been mistaken—or maybe I was. I had thought that the rainforest would be filled with animals, sort of like the St. Louis Zoo, only here the animals could roam freely.

Zac sensed my disappointment. "I'll see if Marcos can take us on a night cruise along the river after dinner," he promised. "The rainforest really comes alive with wildlife at night!"

"But won't it be hard to see?" I asked.

"Not if you use *all* of your senses," Zac said mysteriously.

I wondered what he meant. I mean, if I

couldn't see, then how would I know that the animals were there—and how would I get any pictures? I had told my friends that I was going to see lots of wildlife, and that I'd take photos. But how could I do that if the animals didn't show up? Or if they did, but I couldn't see them?

I swatted the bugs that buzzed in my ear and was glad that I had put on a triple layer of insect spray.

"We're making too much noise," Zac said. "The wildlife can hear you coming, especially when you're on foot, and they warn the others. Listen." I cocked my head and heard deep hoots in the distance. "That's the sound of monkeys warning one another that there are humans nearby," he said.

Zac pointed up. Above us a pair of monkeys leaped from tree to tree. I raised my camera and took a burst of shots as the monkeys disappeared into the canopy.

Finally! I couldn't wait to post this on my blog. But when I scrolled through the photos, all I saw were trees. The monkeys had been too fast,

or I had been too slow. I still had nothing to show my classmates.

We stopped so that I could take a drink of water. I was about to sit on a log when I spotted a line of black ants marching across it. That was a close call! I focused my lens and began snapping pictures, following the ants down the log, up a tree, and . . . I gasped. If I hadn't seen it through my lens I would have thought it was a mountain of dirt, but up close I could see hundreds—no, thousands . . . maybe millions!—of ants. The mountain of ants was about as tall as Tomás. This was something to blog about!

Buoyed by my find, I grabbed a stick and handed it to Zac. "You know what would be cool?" I asked, breathless with excitement. "Take this stick and poke the anthill. And when the ants start to go crazy, I'll shoot a video for my blog!" The video would be epic and amazing! Even Dax would be impressed. I raised my camera. "Go ahead, I'm ready," I called to Zac. "Action!"

Zac didn't move. He just stood there with the stick dangling at his side. Maybe he didn't hear me.

"Go for it," I said again. "Any time now."

Through the lens I saw Zac drop the stick and advance toward me. He looked angry.

"What's the matter?" I asked. "Why didn't you poke them?"

"I'm really disappointed in you, Lea," he said sternly, and pushed past me.

What did I do now? I wondered as I watched him walk away.

"I don't get it," I called after him. "They're just ants, Zac!"

He shook his head and stopped to look at me. "*Just ants?* We don't bash an anthill for entertainment. We don't destroy their habitat for a video so you can show off to your friends back home. What were you thinking?"

My face flushed red. I didn't know what to say. I hadn't thought about that.

"Those ants are just going about their own business," he went on. "For us to bother them, to disturb them, is wrong. Not only is it inconsiderate, but they'll think you're attacking them and fight back. Get all of them riled up, and you could have

some serious ant bites. And if they were bullet
ants—which, thankfully, they are not—one bite
could paralyze you—or me!"

"I—I didn't think—" I sputtered.

"Clearly," Zac said, shaking his head.

He turned to head back to the Barroses'
house and I followed, embarrassed and ashamed.
I had just thought it would make a good video.
But I had let Zac down. I had let the rainforest
down. I had let myself down.

When we got back to the house, Zac went
inside without a word.

I wandered down to the dock and dangled
my feet in the water, feeling alone and naive and
totally out of my element. A couple of small boats
passed, and when the passengers waved, I waved
back, grateful for the friendly gesture. But clearly,
I didn't belong here.

After a while, I headed back toward the
house. I'd e-mail Abby and Camila, I decided, and
maybe even try to video-chat with Mom and Dad.

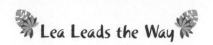

That would make me feel better.

But as I neared the front door I heard a familiar crowing sound. *Great.* Galo Louco was heading toward me, blocking my way to the house. Not knowing what else to do, I scrambled up the gnarled tree that Tomás had used as a hiding place.

Urrgg! I am such a totally clueless city girl, I thought as I straddled a low, sturdy branch. *Enemy to the ants, scared of a chicken.* I felt homesick. And embarrassed that I had bragged to my class about all the wild animals I was going to see—and ashamed that my bragging had driven me to consider destroying the ants' home. A few tears streamed down my cheeks, and I didn't bother to wipe them away. It felt good to cry, and I was glad no one was around to see my pity party.

After a few minutes, I thought I heard someone say my name. I looked down, but no one was there. All I saw was Galo Louco strutting around the tree trunk—and he wasn't talking.

"Lea," the voice said again.

I looked up.

Tomás waved at me shyly from his perch on a higher branch. He wore a crown made from the leaves of a palm frond. He climbed down to a branch near mine and looked at me with curiosity.

"Por que você está chorando?" he asked, running his fingers down his cheeks to signal tears.

I pointed to the chicken and shrugged, wiping the tears from my face. I was certain he was going to laugh at me. But instead, Tomás pulled a piece of fruit out of his pocket. He threw it past Galo Louco, who went running after it.

Then Tomás took the crown off his head and handed it to me.

"Obrigada," I said, feeling better.

"De nada," he said.

I put the crown on my head, and when Tomás smiled, so did I.

Night Cruise
Chapter 8

As the day wore on, I still felt awkward around my brother. I was so ashamed of my behavior with the ants that I couldn't even look at him. At dinner, we didn't say much to each other. Olivia and Marcos were busy chatting and didn't seem to notice. But Tomás sat between us and kept glancing back and forth at Zac and me.

"So, Lea," Marcos said, pushing away from the table, "Zac mentioned you might be up for a night cruise on the river?"

I looked up from my plate where I had been poking at my food, and smiled. "Yes!" I glanced at Zac, but he didn't take his eyes off his meal. I was glad that he had kept his promise and asked Marcos to take us out on the boat.

Even though I could hardly wait to get back on

the river, I did my best not to rush through the rest of my meal. After we packed away the leftovers and cleaned the dishes, we went out to the dock.

In the canoe, I sat up front near Marcos while my brother sat with Olivia and Tomás toward the rear, leaving several rows of seats between us. After cruising along at a high speed, Marcos cut the motor and let the canoe drift silently. It was eerie and beautiful at the same time. The bright moon reminded me of the night in Praia Tropical when we watched the baby turtles hatching from their shells and making their way toward the welcoming waves of the ocean. I wondered how the hatchlings were doing and how many had made it to safety.

Tomás started singing quietly. *"Brilha, brilha, estrelinha ..."* I recognized the tune and realized that he was singing "Twinkle, Twinkle, Little Star" in Portuguese. After a while, Tomás finished his song and we were silent again. Marcos used an oar to slow the boat and let the current carry us.

"I don't see any animals," I whispered to Marcos.

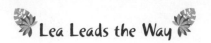

I could see Marcos's smile in the moonlight.
"To know the rainforest is not just to see it, but
to hear it," he whispered. "Close your eyes," he
instructed. I did as I was told. "Now listen. Listen.
Listen."

I expected to hear the hoots of monkeys
that I had heard in the forest earlier that day.
But instead I just heard a constant high-pitched,
pulsing hum.

"What is that buzzing sound?"

"Those are millions of cicadas," Marcos
replied. "Keep listening. Try to listen *deeper*."

Listen *deeper*? What did he mean? I closed
my eyes tight and I tried hard to listen. I wanted
to hear what he was talking about so badly.

"Relax, Lea," Marcos said softly. "This is not
a test. Just relax and listen."

I hadn't realized that my shoulders had
tensed. I exhaled—and that's when I began to
hear it. Softly at first, then more clearly through
the droning cicadas: a glorious symphony of
sounds wafting through the warm Amazon air.
Tree frogs, night birds, the splashes of animals

entering the water. As the wildlife conversation rose all around us, Marcos taught me to isolate each animal's unique sound. The hoots and squawks of owls, the creaking croak of tree frogs, the flutter of wings, and caimans splashing in the water. How could I have missed all this before? It was beautiful, and even though I was in the canoe with others, I felt as if the wildlife were serenading me alone.

I looked at Zac, wanting to tell him how much I loved this. But I knew we were supposed to stay quiet.

"It is so hot in the rainforest that most animals sleep during the day," Marcos explained in a low voice. "When it cools off at night, that's when they come out."

He picked up a flashlight and turned it on. I was surprised by the strong beam of red light. "A regular flashlight would disturb the animals, but this red light lets us see them without bothering them."

He swept the powerful light along the shore. I could see lots of small flashes of red in the trees

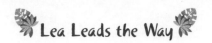

above us and on the riverbank just a few yards away.

"What are those flashes?" I asked.

"Animals' eyes, reflecting the red light," he explained.

I sat up, alert. The animals were so close!

Marcos trained the light far up into a tree. I could see four sets of glowing red eyes. I strained to get a better look.

"It's a family of sloths," he said.

My breath caught in my chest. There they were, their lanky arms clutching the tree branches. Sloths! I longed to see them up close.

We continued down the river, and Marcos slowed the canoe. "This is a favorite spot for caimans," he whispered. "Like most animals, they have very sharp hearing. If we make any sudden noises, they'll swim away. We aren't nearly as interesting to them as they are to us."

With the canoe drifting near shore, Marcos swept the area with his flashlight. Dozens of small red lights lit up, some in the water, some on land. Caimans! My heart leapt with joy—and

a little fear. "How sturdy is the canoe?" I whispered, my voice unsteady.

Marcos let out a low chuckle. "Very sturdy," he said. "We're not going to tip over, Lea. I promise."

Marcos paddled toward shore where the caimans had been, and we heard splashes.

"Are you sure this is a good idea?" I asked.

Marcos nodded. "They're long gone," he said, positioning the canoe against a tangle of trees and brush. He took out a long metal stick with a hook on the end and reached it into the leaves. Suddenly he turned and looked at me. "Are you ready?" he asked.

"For what?" I said.

He pulled the pole out of the tree to reveal ... an anaconda! It was huge. I mean, HUGE. I slapped my hands over my mouth to stifle a scream.

"Don't worry," Marcos assured me. "I won't let him near you. But while I have him here, do you want to take a picture?"

A picture. Yes, a picture. Trembling, I reached for my camera.

"Don't use the flash," Zac called out in a loud

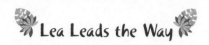

whisper. "There's enough light from the moon."

I got my shots, enough to satisfy Dax, and put my camera down. Marcos released the snake into the water and it slithered away.

As we canoed back to the house, my heart felt a bit lighter. Zac and Marcos were right. The animals had been there the entire time. I just had to be patient.

I moved to one of the middle seats in the canoe and motioned for Zac to join me.

I exhaled. "About this afternoon," I began.

"Later," Zac said. "Let's just enjoy this moment." He put his arm around me. It felt right.

We were both quiet for the longest time, looking at the stars, listening to the wildlife. But then I felt two little hands pushing us apart and Tomás sat down between us. He smiled up at me, and then turned his grin on Zac. Then the three of us broke into a laugh that echoed across the river.

Wildlife Encounters

Chapter 9

The next morning, I awoke to a gentle pitter-patter sound. I stretched out my arms as I yawned. Then my eyes flew open and I rushed to the window. It was raining. Did that mean that Zac and I couldn't go on another rainforest hike today?

Once I was dressed, I went into the kitchen and found everybody doing their daily morning chores. Zac was setting the table, Olivia was cooking, Marcos sliced the fresh fruit, and Tomás helped carry the food to the table. I assumed that I was expected to help, too. I wouldn't have minded—after all, I had lots of chores at home, like doing the dishes, raking the leaves in the fall, and helping shovel snow in the winter—but those chores weren't fraught with danger. Leaving the kitchen, I took a deep breath to prepare myself for another Galo Louco attack. I was about to head outside to the henhouse when Tomás came through the front door, his hair dripping wet with rain, and handed me a basket full of eggs.

"Obrigada!" I exclaimed.

Tomás gave me a shy smile, and we walked into the kitchen together.

When we had finished setting the table, Olivia told us it would be a few more minutes until breakfast. "You two relax for a bit," she told us. "I'll let you know when breakfast is ready."

I followed Zac into the living room and we sat next to each other on the couch.

"Zac, I am so sorry about what happened with the ants yesterday," I blurted, wanting to get it off my chest. "I was careless and selfish and, well . . . you were right. I was thinking more about getting a great video than how that would affect the ants and their habitat."

Zac looked at me. "And I shouldn't have gotten so mad at you," he confessed. "It's just that I care about the wildlife in the rainforest and I'd do anything to protect it." He sighed. "I just wish I

could do more—and I still have a lot to learn."

"Me too," I said.

Zac put his arm around my shoulder and gave me a squeeze. "I'll tell you what, Lea. When the rain lets up, let's take the rowboat out on the water. I know a place down the river where a bunch of monkey families hang out. I bet you could get some great photos for your blog there."

"I'd like that," I said. I looked out the window. If only there were an off switch for the rain!

But the rain kept pouring, well past lunch. While Tomás and Macaco, his stuffed monkey, watched the rainfall from his bedroom window, I opened Ama's travel journal. I'd hardly had a chance to read it since I arrived in the rainforest.

Not long after her trip to Alaska, Ama went to Tanzania, where she visited an animal rescue center:

It was love at first sight when I saw Georgie, a skinny young giraffe with a cast on his long leg. I

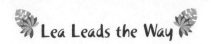

was told that he had been injured while fleeing a lion attack. Georgie's mother hadn't survived the attack, so he had been orphaned.

We bonded quickly, and he followed me everywhere. I wanted so badly to take Georgie home, but I knew that was impossible. Imagine, a giraffe in my tiny house! But I hated the thought of leaving him behind. I wanted to do what I could to help him survive and thrive on the savanna. That's when I decided to adopt him! Well, not in the literal sense of the word. But I made a plan to donate some money to help pay for his food and medical bills.

It was hard to say good-bye to Georgie, but knowing that he was in good hands was a comfort. And knowing that I had made a new friend—one with very long legs!—warmed my heart.

I closed Ama's journal and felt a rush of impatience. I couldn't wait to get back outside to see some more animals.

I sat at the small table next to Tomás's bed and worked on a blog post about my hike in the rainforest and the night cruise. I was pleased that Zac was in the background of the photo of the ant mountain so that my friends could get an idea of how big it really was.

The minute I posted my blog, comments and questions about the rainforest started pouring in from my classmates. (There was only a one-hour time difference between here and St. Louis, I realized, which meant that it was library hour.) Even Dax was impressed by my photos of the ant mountain—and especially the anaconda.

Then I moved on to my e-mails. I was excited to hear from Camila, who told me that her family was planning a trip to Chicago in April.

Quickly, I wrote back. *The drive from Chicago to St. Louis isn't very far! And I'll be on spring break for a week in April! Fingers crossed that you can visit me then!!!*

I e-mailed Mom and Dad to be sure that Camila was invited, and Mom got right back and assured me that she was. She also reported that

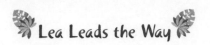
my father was going a little stir-crazy from not being able to go anywhere because of his broken leg—but that she was surfing up a storm.

Tomás brought out a big bin of crayons and some paper and sat next to me, propping up Macaco in his own chair. I watched as Tomás began to draw the river and the trees along the banks. Then he drew an outline of a dolphin under the water. As he rooted around his bin, I spotted a gray crayon and handed it to him. He shook his head, instead reaching for a pink one.

What an imagination! I thought as he colored the dolphin pink. Next he drew a kitten—or maybe it was a leopard since it had spots. I chose some brightly colored crayons and handed them to Tomás, thinking that a purple-and-green leopard would go well with his pink dolphin, but instead he reached for yellow and brown and black.

Olivia appeared in the doorway. She squatted down next to the table to look at Tomás's drawing. "*Bom trabalho!* Good job, Tomás." She turned to me. "He sure loves margays."

What's a margay? I wondered.

I typed "margay" into my web browser and there was the animal Tomás was drawing, right on my screen! It looked like a leopard, but smaller, with little rounded ears and huge brown eyes.

Tomás looked over my shoulder at the margays on the screen. He pointed to one and then to his picture.

"It's the same," I said, nodding. "Margay!"

Just then, Zac popped into the room and said in a fake stern voice, "Lea! What are you doing sitting around when you could be cruising down the Amazon River?"

I looked outside. The rain had stopped and the sun was shining!

The rain left a clean fresh scent in the air. Zac led me to a small, faded green rowboat on the other side of the dock from where Marcos kept his big canoe tied up. The rowboat looked as if it could barely float. When I boarded, it rocked back and forth, and I quickly sat down so as not to go for another unscheduled swim.

Zac was an expert with the oars, and soon we were skimming along the river, flanked on either side by lush forests. The trees were still dripping and steaming, the leaves shiny and sparkling from all the rain. Brightly colored parrots flew overhead and perched high in the tree branches. I took out my camera, zoomed in, and got some great photos.

"Look!" Zac said. He pointed to the water just a few feet away.

I wasn't sure if what I was seeing was real. It took my breath away.

"A dolphin!" I cried. But it wasn't just any dolphin—it was a *bubblegum pink* dolphin, just like the one Tomás had drawn!

"That's a *boto*, a freshwater dolphin," Zac said as he slowed the rowboat. "When the water level is low, you'll see more of them around here."

The boto glided in and out of the water. I glimpsed a second, smaller flash of pink beside her.

"Look!" I exclaimed. "There are two of them. Is that her baby?"

Zac grinned and nodded. I took some photos,

and then began to record a video. My heart fluttered at the sight of the two of them together.

"What's she doing?" I asked as the mother boto nudged her baby.

"She's teaching her calf to come up for air as he swims," Zac said.

"Her *calf*? Zac—it's a baby boto, not a baby cow!"

Zac smiled. "That's what baby dolphins and botos are called. Calves."

The botos swam beside us as we glided down the river. Before long, Zac started steering us toward the shore, and the botos continued on their way.

The bottom of the boat dragged along the shallow riverbed, and we came to a gentle stop. Zac hopped out, tugged the boat onto the shore, and gave me his hand to help me up. After just a few steps, we found ourselves in the dense greenery of the rainforest.

The leaves stirred above me, and I was able to get several photos of monkeys swinging through the branches. I got one great shot of a monkey in

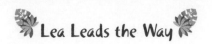

midair as he leapt from tree to tree.

We ducked under a low branch, and I spotted a giant spider on it. At home, I normally screamed when I saw spiders. This time, I took photos of it instead.

As we walked, I thought about the questions my classmates had asked on my blog. I had been getting a great response to each post, but since Ms. Swain had offered extra credit to anyone who asked me a question about Brazil that I answered, my inbox was flooded.

I read that a lot of rainforest animals are endangered, Abby had written. *What is causing them to die out?*

I wasn't sure, so I asked Zac.

"The animals here face many threats, but one big problem is poachers," Zac said matter-of-factly.

Poachers? Didn't poaching have something to do with eggs? "What are poachers?" I asked.

"People who kidnap animals and sell them as pets. Every year, the rainforest loses over ten million animals to poachers."

"Ten million?" I exclaimed. "That's awful."

"Deforestation is also a problem," he continued. "Cattle ranchers and farmers clear the land for their farms, and loggers cut down trees to sell the wood—trees that were once the homes of many animals. Imagine if someone came to St. Louis and began to destroy all the homes in Lafayette Square. What would we do? Where would we live?"

I shrugged and shook my head, feeling helpless and horrified. *Where would the animals go if the trees weren't here?* My heart ached when I thought about all the animals that had been kidnapped and sold away by poachers, and the poor birds, monkeys, and even spiders and insects that had lost their homes in the trees.

We continued to walk in silence. After a while, we came into a small clearing. Zac went to inspect a large millipede that was squirming up a tree trunk. I kept my distance, but zoomed in my camera lens for a good shot. Then I panned around us, taking photos of the lush rainforest. The forest floor was covered with leaves, and when I looked closely I could see armies of ants

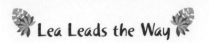

and other insects scurrying every which way.
Then I spotted something strange on my camera screen. Slowly I lowered the camera. On the
ground ahead of me was a small pile of matted
fur in the leaves. At first I thought it was a stuffed
animal or—my breath caught—a dead one. But
then I saw that it was breathing. As I approached,
I could see that it was moving one of its arms very
slowly. It had long black-and-white fur, and was
curled up in the leaves—

I gasped.

"Zac!" I called out. "Zac, it's a baby sloth!"

A Fateful Discovery

Chapter 10

Cautiously, I walked around the little sloth. It hardly moved, but then sloths are known to be slow-moving. Still, there was a knot in my stomach, and I had a feeling that something was wrong. Why was it all alone? Had it fallen out of the tree? Was it hurt?

Zac ran over to me. We both bent down. The sloth let go of a heartbreaking sound that I will never forget. It was a weak bleating noise, like a baby goat.

"It's very young," he said.

"We have to help it!" I pleaded.

Zac stood up. "Lea, you stay with the sloth. I'll scout around. Mothers rarely stray far away from their babies. Don't touch it, though. We don't want to get our scent on it."

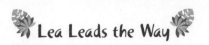
As I stood guard over the sloth, I bent down and spoke softly to it. "Everything's going to be okay. I'm right here with you."

The little sloth lay on its stomach at the base of a tall tree. It was the sweetest thing I had ever seen. Brown fur framed its friendly white face and dark eyes, and it had a tiny black nose. And even though its mouth was turned up in a smile, the frightened look in its eyes told me it wasn't happy. Its breathing seemed shallow, and although it tried, it was too weak to crawl away. It smelled sort of bad, but I stayed close. Nothing could keep me away from this baby sloth.

Soon my brother returned. He looked distressed.

"Did you find the mother?" I asked.

Zac shook his head. "No sign of her," he reported. He ran his hand through his mop of brown hair.

"What does that mean?" I asked. I thought of the boto mother who took such good care of her calf. Where was this sloth's mother?

"Most likely, the baby lost its grip on its

mother and she wasn't able to rescue her baby. Or something bad may have happened to the mother. Maybe a predator attacked her or a poacher took her."

Worry set in. I looked down at the helpless baby sloth. "So what else can we do? We have to save it, Zac!"

He released a big sigh. "Okay, let me see if I can get it to latch on to the tree. It'll be safer there."

I nodded.

Gently, Zac picked up the baby sloth. I followed and took photos as he tried to get the sloth to latch. Slowly, instinctively, the creature reached out and tried to wrap its weak arms around the branch. It trembled and let out another cry. But as hard as it tried, it couldn't hold on to the branch.

Zac gathered the baby close to him and it clung to his shoulder as he inspected one of its front paws. "Come here," he said. "Look."

I peered at the baby's small paws, which had long toes, or fingers, almost like hands. A couple of its claws were broken off.

"This is a three-toed sloth," Zac explained.

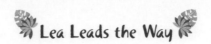

"I think its broken claws are part of the reason that it can't latch on."

"Will the sloth be able to live on its own out here?" I asked. "It'll be okay, right?"

"I'm afraid it's too little to fend off predators and too weak to search for food. The missing claws will make it impossible to climb, and at this age, it has no sense of direction, so it's easy prey."

"Maybe we could bring it back to the Barroses' house," I suggested. "We'll nurse it back to health, and then I can adopt it!" I knew a thing or two about taking care of animals in need. I always helped whenever Abby's family took in rescue animals from the local shelter. And last year at school I found a baby sparrow that had fallen from a nest. We fed him by hand, and he became our class bird. We named him Tweety. Maybe we could have a class sloth, too!

"I'm sorry, Lea. That's just not possible. Besides, it would be illegal for you to take a sloth out of the rainforest," Zac said, bringing me back to reality with a thud.

I bit my lip. "Then maybe Olivia and Marcos

will be able to take care of it."

Zac shook his head. "To nurse this baby back to health would be a full-time job. They already have their hands full with Tomás and their jobs."

"Well, I could do it!" I volunteered.

"Lea, you leave in three days."

"What about you?" I said, scrambling for solutions. "You've got another half a year here."

"Yes, but I have my research and studies, which will start up again next week," Zac reminded me. "Besides, I'm not trained in wildlife rescue or rehabilitation. Caring for a wild animal, especially one this young, is very difficult."

"But—" I started. But *what?* I knew he was right. My voice trembled. "May I hold it?"

When Zac put the baby in my arms, my body flooded with love for it. Was this how mothers felt when they cuddled their babies? The sloth clung to me, resting its tiny head on my shoulder. It weighed almost nothing. How could I leave this little baby sloth to die alone in the rainforest? I began to sob. I felt so helpless.

Zac looked miserable. "I know this hurts," he

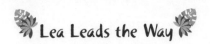

said gently. "Mother Nature can be cruel. I'm so sorry, Lea. But this sort of thing happens a thousand times a day in the rainforest."

"But it doesn't happen a thousand times a day to *this* baby," I blubbered. "Maybe I can't stop the poachers or bring the trees back on my own. But Zac, I want to save this baby. You said you wanted to give back to the rainforest. Well, here's your chance to help—one animal at a time."

By the way he set his jaw, I could tell that Zac was thinking hard about what I had said. He let out a deep sigh, and then his eyes lit up. "I have a professor who specializes in wildlife rehabilitation. I don't have her phone number, but I can e-mail her and see if she has any recommendations. But I can't make any promises, okay?"

I nodded, then got teary again, this time with happiness. Maybe there was hope for this baby sloth after all.

Tomás was up in his tree when Zac and I returned to the Barroses' house with the little sloth. He quickly scrambled down and looked curiously at the creature sleeping in my arms.

"*Mãe!*" he called, and ran inside to get his mother.

Olivia rushed out and inspected the baby sloth. "Poor girl. She's probably dehydrated and hungry," she said. She turned to Zac. "Take the canoe down the river to the third house. You know, the blue one with the red trim on the windows. They have goats. We'll need some goat's milk right away."

As she said this, I realized how little I knew about taking care of a sick sloth. Sure, I had helped nurse Tweety back to health. And I have been taking care of my turtle Ginger for the past five years. But she lives in a glass aquarium with a water filter and lights, and I can buy her food at the pet store just down the street. I had no idea what to do to help an injured baby sloth.

I held the baby closer, careful not to squeeze her too tight, and gently stroked her fur. Tomás stood quietly by my side, and then started to sing a slow song in Portuguese that sounded like a lullaby. He leaned over to nuzzle the sloth's soft head, but stopped. He pointed to the baby and held his nose. I had grown used to her smell by now and didn't mind it.

In a little while, Zac returned with the goat's milk. Olivia found an eyedropper and filled it with milk. I tried to give the sloth to Zac to feed her, but she wouldn't let go of me. So I held on to her as Zac brought the eyedropper to her mouth. She eagerly took the goat's milk, and my heart soared.

I thought of the times when Mom or Ama had said to me, "Eat! You should eat more!" And now, here I was, thinking the same thing.

Almost immediately after eating, the sloth fell asleep. I sat on the couch, not wanting to awaken her.

Zac sat down next to me. "I e-mailed my professor," he said.

"What did she say?" I asked.

Zac shook his head. "Haven't heard back yet. We've done all we can for now. The next step is to wait."

I had no idea waiting could be so hard.

Marcos found an empty wooden fruit crate, and I asked Tomás to hold the sloth while I went outside to gather some leaves to cushion the bottom of the crate.

Once the sloth's bed was ready, I joined Olivia, Marcos, and Zac in the living room, where Tomás was still cradling the baby. I smiled and took some pictures. Suddenly, Ama popped into my mind. How I would have loved to share a moment like this with her! I missed my grandmother so much just then. I would have given anything to hug her and to tell her about the baby sloth that we had found in the rainforest.

This little baby was all alone in the world. That's when I decided that I'd give her a name. *But what name would be worthy of this brave little girl?* I asked myself. Then it hit me.

"I think we should name her Amanda," I announced.

Zac smiled at me. "After Ama," he said, nodding. He turned to Tomás and translated into Portuguese.

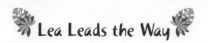
Tomás smiled. "Amanda," he said, then whispered the name in her ear.

That night, I couldn't wait to blog about Amanda. My classmates would be so excited to hear about how I had found her in the rainforest, and I knew that once they saw the photos they would fall in love with Amanda, too.

Tomás sat nearby, cradling the baby sloth as I wrote:

Today we found a baby sloth. She's injured and in poor shape. Sloths, especially babies, are always in danger because they move so slowly. We were lucky to find this little one on the ground before a predator did. Although, sometimes other animals don't even notice sloths because they are so still! Sloths eat and sleep and even give birth hanging upside down from tree branches. But Amanda is missing some claws and has trouble gripping. I can only hope that we can find her the help she needs

to gain her strength back and learn how to
survive in the wild.

When I was done writing, it was time for bed.
I gently placed Amanda in her bed. Tomás looked
on and furrowed his brow.

"*O que?*" I asked him. "What is it, Tomás?"

He held up his hand for me to wait and then
ran down the hall. When he returned, Macaco
was in his arms. He gave his stuffed monkey a
big hug, and then gently placed him in the crate
next to Amanda. With great effort she wrapped
herself around Macaco and snuggled up to him.

My heart nearly burst with love. I gave Tomás
two thumbs-up and he returned the gesture. Then
together we watched over Amanda until she fell
asleep.

Amanda

Chapter 11

I dreamed that I was hiking in the rainforest with Zac. Amanda was on the ground, helpless and crying, but I walked right past her and kept going. When I realized what I had done, I turned around. But she was gone...

I awoke in a sweat. It was still dark outside. I immediately went to check on Amanda in her crate, but she wasn't there. I panicked for a moment—had she escaped? Had somebody taken her? Then I saw the light on in the kitchen.

"Lea, bom dia," Marcos said, looking up at me. He was sitting at the dining room table cradling the baby sloth in one arm and feeding her from the dropper.

I felt my body relax as my breathing slowed down. *Phew!* Amanda was safe.

"Babies need to eat often," Marcos explained as he dipped the dropper into a glass of goat's milk. "Their stomachs are small, so they need to eat lots of little meals."

I nodded, recalling that when Abby's little brother was a baby, it seemed like he was being fed all the time.

Marcos shifted and handed Amanda to me. "Why don't you finish feeding her?" he said. "I've got to get ready for a daybreak river tour."

I took Amanda, who looked drowsy. It felt great to hold her again. "Isn't it awfully early for a tour?" I asked him.

"The sunrise over the Amazon River is a sight unlike any other," Marcos said, after taking a long sip of coffee. "It's worth getting up extra early for. I'll take you before you leave," he promised.

Before I leave . . .

In a few days my parents would fly to Manaus to meet me, and then together we'd travel back home to Lafayette Square, my neighborhood in St. Louis. I thought back to when I

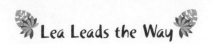

had first arrived in the Amazon, when I felt out of place and homesick. I looked down at Amanda, who was sleeping soundly. Now I couldn't imagine leaving the rainforest. I couldn't imagine leaving Amanda behind.

After Marcos left, I got out my tablet and logged on to my blog while Amanda napped nearby in her crate. I wanted to stay as close to her as possible. Even though she had been drinking the goat milk, she seemed to be getting weaker, and this worried me.

I had a lot of comments on my blog. As I scrolled through the posts, I smiled. Everyone loved the botos, although a couple of the boys accused me of photoshopping the picture to turn the river dolphins pink. And most of my classmates had commented about Amanda. It seemed that they were as smitten with her as I was.

JESSA: She's so cute!

Ms. SWAIN: How lucky that you found her!

EMILIA: Oooh, I want a sloth as a pet!

LUCA: Is her fur soft or prickly?

Dax: Cool! You should bring her home to St. Louis.
Jayden: Is Amanda going to live???

Then I read this:

Abby: Really, Lea? I can't believe you took that
sloth out of her natural habitat!

I gasped. Of everyone in my class, I thought
Abby would have been the happiest with what I
had done! Suddenly it felt like a weight had been
dropped on me. I couldn't believe that Abby had
accused me of doing something wrong. Amanda
needed our help—couldn't Abby see that?

I bent over Amanda's crate to check on her.
She was even more lethargic than just fifteen
minutes ago when I had finished feeding her.
She looked up at me and let out a weak cry.

I gathered Amanda in my arms and ran
into Zac's room. "Zac? Zac!" I said, rousting him
awake. "I think Amanda's getting worse. Can
you check to see if your professor has gotten
back to you yet?"

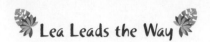
He sat up and rubbed his eyes. Without a word, he logged on to his laptop. "Nothing yet," he reported. "But it's only 6 a.m. She's probably still asleep. We need to be patient."

"But Zac," I cried, "I'm not sure how much longer she'll last without help. I'm so scared."

He peered at Amanda and sighed. "I'm worried about her, too."

As we sat down to breakfast, I put the crate between Tomás and me. Amanda slept next to Macaco, too weak to hug him. Olivia brought out freshly baked cheese rolls, but Tomás, Zac, and I didn't have much of an appetite. We ate quietly, spending more time watching the baby sloth than eating our meals. Zac kept his laptop on the table so that he would know right away when his professor responded to his e-mail.

When his computer pinged, everyone turned and looked at it. Zac set down his glass of papaya juice and immediately checked his e-mail.

"Good news," Zac finally said, beaming.

Amanda

"Professor Da Rocha says there's a wildlife sanctuary about an hour from here. They specialize in wild animal rescue and rehabilitation."

"So they'll take Amanda?" I asked hopefully.

"I'm not sure if they'll have enough room or resources," Zac said. "But I'll call them right away." He pulled his cell phone out of his pocket and dialed the number on his screen.

As Zac spoke to the sanctuary worker, he nodded solemnly and kept glancing at Amanda. At one point he held up her claws and examined them, speaking rapidly in Portuguese.

I held my breath. This could be Amanda's only chance for survival. What would happen if the sanctuary wouldn't take her?

"Obrigado," Zac said and hung up the call.

"Well?" I asked.

"They said to bring her in. She'll get an exam, and then they'll decide if they can help her." Zac turned to Olivia. "May I take the truck?"

Olivia nodded. "They'll know what's best for Amanda," she said with a warm look at me.

I gave Olivia a hopeful smile and then leaned

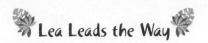

over Amanda's crate. "We're going to try to get you help," I whispered.

The hour-long drive felt like forever. Tomás and I took turns holding Amanda. She wouldn't—or maybe couldn't—drink anymore. She hardly moved and couldn't even lift her head. I blinked back tears.

As we drove, Zac tried to assure me that Amanda would be okay. "The sanctuary workers will know what's best for her. The only place she'd be safer is with her own mother."

That got me thinking about Abby's accusation. Questions tumbled over and over in my head. Was I wrong to take Amanda out of the rainforest? What if her mother came back for her and realized she was missing? Was I as bad as the poachers? On the other hand, what would have happened to Amanda had we not found her and taken her home? I looked at little Amanda, and my throat tightened.

I was about to ask Zac if I had done the right thing, but then I thought about how hard I had tried to convince him to help me save her. I couldn't tell him now that I was questioning our choice.

Wildlife Sanctuary

Chapter 12

A friendly woman with cropped blonde hair accented with a swatch of pink greeted us at the Amazonas Wildlife Sanctuary. "Olá! Hello," she said, extending her hand and shaking Zac's as Tomás gripped Macaco and hid behind me. "I'm Erika, the director of the wildlife sanctuary. You must be Zac. Professor Da Rocha told me to expect you. She says you're one of her best students. I was an exchange student myself before I settled here in Brazil. Nice to meet you in person!"

Zac returned the handshake and then introduced Tomás and me.

"Muito prazer," I said. "This is Amanda." I turned so that she could see Amanda's little face over my shoulder.

"May I?" she asked, reaching out to Amanda.

Reluctantly, I handed her over. Erika's friendly blue eyes got serious. "She doesn't look well," she said. "Please, follow me this way."

Erika guided us into a room that looked like a doctor's office. She gently set Amanda on a metal table and listened to her heart with a stethoscope. Tomás held both Zac's and my hands as we all watched silently. Erika inspected Amanda's fur, looked in her mouth and ears, and took a blood sample. Amanda was very brave and did not cry. I remembered being afraid to go to the doctor's office when I was little. But I always got a sticker at the end for being brave.

Finally Erika handed Amanda back to me, and then wrote some things down on a chart.

"She's very lucky that you found her when you did," she began. "Her injuries are consistent with a fall from a high place, and she has a fractured leg. From the look of her wounds, I would guess that she was attacked by a harpy eagle. Did you see her mother when you found her?"

Zac and I both shook our heads.

Erika pursed her lips. "It's possible that she

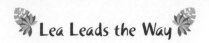

wasn't as lucky as her baby."

"You mean—" I began.

"Most likely the eagle made off with the mother."

I was silent as tears welled in my eyes. How terrifying that must have been for Amanda and her mother . . .

"Baby sloths hold on to their mothers until they are about eight months old," Erika continued. "I would venture that this little girl is about five or six months old. If they were being attacked, it's likely that Amanda let go. It looks like her wounds are quite infected. If they go untreated, she could die."

I gasped. "Do you think you can treat her?"

"Yes, I think so," she said. "The good news is that antibiotics ought to clear up the infection in a few days. The bad news is that her leg will take much longer to heal, and a couple of her claws are broken, probably from the fall."

"But Amanda's going to be all right, isn't she?" I asked. "Will she eventually be able to return to the rainforest?" Maybe Abby would see that I had done the right thing if I could just tell her that Amanda would return home.

Erika shrugged. "I can't make any promises. But I'll tell you what: You can leave Amanda here with us for now. We'll give her medicine and monitor her for the next couple of days. If she pulls through, then we'll come up with the best plan for her."

I bit my lip and nodded. I couldn't imagine leaving Amanda, but I knew she would be in good hands here.

Erika smiled. "Amanda needs a bath. Do I have any volunteers to help me?" She repeated her question in Portuguese for Tomás. He came out from behind me and raised his hand.

Erika filled two blue plastic tubs with warm water. She dipped Amanda in the shallow water of the first tub and showed Tomás and me how to gently wash her with baby shampoo, making sure to be careful with her fractured leg. Then we moved her to the second tub. Erika dropped a handful of leaves and flowers into the water. It smelled like a fragrant tea.

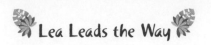

"This will keep Amanda parasite-free and smelling good," Erika explained as we rubbed the leaves and tea into her fur.

I gingerly lifted Amanda out of the bath. Erika wrapped her in a soft yellow towel. "Normally, we hang our sloths up to dry in the sun," she said, pointing to a couple of sloths clinging to branches nearby. "But since Amanda's claws are damaged, we are going to have to *teach* her how to hang on. For now, we'll dry her with this." Tomás's eyes widened when she pulled out a blow-dryer. Zac held Amanda as Erika dried her, so I could take pictures.

Amanda looked so cute and fluffy when she was done with her spa treatment. I held her and buried my nose in her fur. She sure smelled better than she had when we arrived at the sanctuary. "You're beautiful," I told her. "But then, you always were."

Zac turned to Tomás. "Should we give you a bath next?" he asked in Portuguese, and then again in English. Tomás giggled and offered up Macaco in his place.

Next, Erika set Amanda's injured back leg in a small cast. "This way the bones will fuse correctly," she explained.

Zac nudged me. "She looks like Dad."

I giggled, remembering how Dad had hobbled around in his cast back in Praia Tropical. I took photos to share with him.

Erika finished the cast and applied some antibacterial ointment on Amanda's wounds. "Now, this baby has been an excellent patient. I have something for her."

A sticker! I mused. And I was right, sort of. Erika gave Amanda a hibiscus flower. *That's so cute,* I thought. *A sloth version of a sticker that she can play with.* But I was wrong. Instead, the flower was to eat!

"Sloths love these," Erika said. "They're a real sweet treat." Amanda nibbled on the flower slowly and happily.

Later, while Amanda napped, Erika gave us a tour. I was expecting that the sanctuary would look like a zoo, with penned-off areas for the animals. But I was surprised to see that most of the animals roamed free—although they did keep natural enemies separated. Monkeys scampered on couches, birds perched on the backs of chairs, and sloths hung upside down from a wooden pole that looked like the ballet barre I used to practice on when I was little.

Half a dozen volunteers and sanctuary personnel were bathing and feeding the animals. I watched a young man running after the most enormous guinea pig I had ever seen. It was as big as a dog!

"What is that?" I asked.

Erika chuckled. "That's Clara the capybara. Capybaras are the biggest rodents in the world." I took a quick photo to post to my blog.

Erika let me feed some passion fruit to a toucan named Tiago. When he was done, he let out a loud squawk. "That's toucan for 'thank you!'" Erika said.

Next, I got to hold a tiny monkey the size of my thumb. "Her name is Beatriz and she's a pygmy marmoset," Erika told me.

I laughed as the little monkey scrambled

up my arm. "This place is better than any zoo I've ever been to!" I told Erika. "Do you get a lot of visitors here?"

"We're different from a zoo," Erika said. "The animals that find their way here are sick or injured, so it's our job to rehabilitate them and return them to the rainforest. Also, zoos often charge an admission to see the animals. Here, we rely on donations and fund-raisers to take care of the animals. I wish we could take in all the animals that need our help, but we can't afford to. We don't have the space, the staff, or the resources. Still, we do what we can with what we have."

Suddenly, I heard Tomás squeal. He was so excited he almost dropped Macaco. Tomás stood at a window, watching as a volunteer tended to some kittens. But these weren't just any kittens— they were margays! They were so cute with their spotted fur and huge brown eyes. I whipped out my camera. Soon, a staff person brought in the mother margay and let her tend to her babies. The mother's fur was thick and plush, and she had spots like a leopard. Her babies snuggled

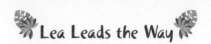

close to her and started nursing.

"Margay sightings are very rare," Erika told us. "To see one with her kittens is even rarer. These babies are a couple of weeks old and have just recently opened their eyes."

"Why are they here?" I asked. "Were they in danger?"

"The mother was in distress when we discovered her," Erika said. "It was a difficult birth, but we were able to assist and deliver healthy babies. They will all stay here while the mother recovers. When she's better, we'll release the family back into the wild."

Tomás looked so happy as he admired the kittens through the window. The volunteer picked up one of the kittens and brought him closer for Tomás to see. Tomás touched the window and giggled as the kitten batted at his finger through the glass.

Soon enough, it was time to go. My heart was so heavy that it hurt. How could I possibly leave Amanda?

"Can we come back tomorrow?" I begged

Zac. I was choking on my words, trying not to cry.

"Yes," he said, giving me a hug. "Of course, Lea. We'll come back."

I noticed that Tomás was teary, too. We both took turns hugging and kissing Amanda, and then I set her down. As we headed for the truck, Tomás suddenly turned around and ran back toward the sanctuary.

"Tomás! Tomás, what are you doing?" I called out as I chased him. Was he going back to see the baby margays?

When I caught up with Tomás, he was kneeling over Amanda. He had given Macaco to her so that she wouldn't be lonely, and she was hugging the stuffed monkey. When Tomás looked at me, I gave him a thumbs-up. Then, hand in hand, we walked to the truck where Zac was waiting for us.

A Difficult Debate

Chapter 13

When we finally got back to the Barroses' house, the sun was setting. Zac carried a sleeping Tomás inside, and Olivia put him to bed. When I looked at Amanda's empty crate, my heart ached. Without Amanda snuggled next to me, it felt like a part of me was missing.

After dinner, I went to Tomás's room. I was physically and emotionally exhausted, but I knew that my classmates were waiting to get an update on Amanda on my blog. I logged on to my blog site and sure enough, everyone was asking about Amanda. I let them know that she was in good hands, but that her survival was uncertain.

Then, I reread Abby's comment on my last post, the comment that had been bothering me:

Really, Lea? I can't believe you took that sloth out of her natural habitat!

I took a deep breath and started typing a reply:

Hi, Abby. Amanda needed help. I couldn't just leave her there to die. Your mother is a veterinarian and she saves animals' lives every day. How is this different?

I wondered when she would see my post. It was just past dinnertime in St. Louis. Abby was probably doing homework at her desk in her bedroom at this very minute. Still, I was surprised when Abby's reply popped up almost immediately.

ABBY: My mom saves <u>pets'</u> lives. That's the difference. They've been raised by humans. They are domesticated and rely on us for survival. They couldn't last on their own in the wild. But we shouldn't interfere with wild animals.

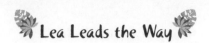

Interfere? Is that what she thought I was doing?

LEA: Remember in third grade when we saved Tweety, the bird who fell from his nest? In order to save him, we had to carry him to safety. You even helped by calling your mom and asking her what we should do. Left alone, Tweety would have died.

ABBY: The Amazon rainforest is different from St. Louis. The animals here are used to sharing their environment with people, and even depend on them to put out birdseed and plant trees in their neighborhoods. But in the rainforest, the cycle of life goes on without our help.

LEA: So are you saying I should have just left an orphaned baby sloth there to die alone?

I stared at the tablet screen, waiting for a reply from Abby. When I didn't see another post for the longest time, at first I was angry, then I

was upset, and then I was sad. It felt awful to be arguing with my best friend.

Finally, another message popped up.

ABBY: I didn't know she was an orphan. Why didn't you tell me?! You only wrote that you found a baby sloth!

I felt stupid—I hadn't done a good job of explaining what was going on. No wonder Abby was upset with me! I quickly replied:

Amanda's mother was probably killed by a harpy eagle. Amanda was helpless and alone. If we hadn't found her, someone—or something— else would have. I don't know if she'll survive at the sanctuary. But I do know it's her only chance for survival.

Abby, I know what you're saying about not interfering with the rainforest, but sadly that's not 100% true. We humans DO interfere: Loggers and ranchers are cutting down the forests,

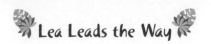

leaving the wild animals with fewer places to
live. And poachers kidnap exotic animals. I wish I
could solve all of these problems. When I found
Amanda, I realized I could help save at least one
animal—so I had to try.

After a few agonizing minutes, Abby finally
replied.

Wow. I didn't realize that all that was going on.
I get now that you did what you had to do to
save that baby sloth. And it sounds like there are
many more animals that need help.

There was a pause, and then she wrote:

What can we do?

I was so happy that Abby finally understood.
Then it occurred to me that my blog was the
reason Abby knew about Amanda's plight—and
now, about the plight of the other animals in the
sanctuary and in the rainforest.

For the first time, I realized that my blog had the potential to make a difference. My classmates all cared. And if each of them told other people and got them to care, who knew what we could accomplish?

Lea: Get the word out! Tell others about the Amazon rainforest. I'm still learning a lot about it, and with this blog, I'll share what I learn. I know that it would be impossible for us to save all the animals, but that doesn't mean we shouldn't try. Even if it's saving just one animal at a time.

Then I posted a picture of Amanda, all fresh and fluffy, and hit "send."

A Gift

Chapter 14

The next day, I sat on Tomás's bed reading all of my classmates' blog comments. They were super excited to help spread the word, and they were already planning some class projects to share information about the rainforest with other classes at Samuel Clemens Elementary.

Tomás sat across the room drawing a picture of Amanda. I was impressed that he had given his beloved Macaco to her yesterday. It reminded me of Ama's rule: When you visit a new place, you should always leave something behind.

But what could I leave behind for the rainforest, which had given me so much? It was here that I had been welcomed into the Barros family and found Amanda. I looked through my suitcase. What good would it do to leave behind a

picture of my pet turtle—or my flip-flops? I had
nothing to give.

Zac stuck his head in the door. "You ready?"

He had told Tomás and me that we could
join him for a trip into town to pick up some
groceries for Olivia. I grabbed my bag, making
sure that I had my wallet. I had saved my birthday money along with my allowance for this trip
and had yet to spend most of it. I was looking
forward to finding something to remind me of
my visit to Brazil. Maybe I'd find a souvenir this
afternoon.

Tomás and Zac ran ahead as I followed them
to the dock. It was faster to take the rowboat than
to walk.

But before I could reach the dock, I heard
a squawk. Galo Louco.

I took several slow steps toward the dock.
Galo Louco strutted toward me, his eyes never
leaving my face. But this time, instead of running, I took a step toward him. It was like a
showdown, each of us determined not to be
the first to look away.

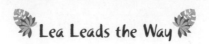

"Lea, let's go!" my brother called from the dock.

"Shhh!" I said. "Just give me a minute."

My heart fluttered as Galo Louco came to a stop right in front of me and tilted his head. I knew he was about to start pecking at my feet, but before he could, I reached into my bag.

"This is for you," I said. Without taking my eyes off him, I pulled out a small banana that I had placed in my bag and waved it at him. "You don't scare me," I told the rooster.

I peeled the banana and broke off several small pieces, tossing them just behind him. Galo Louco looked at the banana and then looked at me. Then he made his choice.

As he happily gobbled up the banana, I stepped past him and made my way to the dock.

Zac stretched out his long legs as he waited for me to get my life jacket on. Tomás sat next to him and did the same. I had to laugh at the two of them sitting side by side, both wearing sunglasses, their hands behind their heads.

Since no one had picked up the oars, I did.

A Gift

I can row a boat, I thought. *How difficult can it be?*

Very difficult, it turned out. After watching me struggle, Zac helped me push off and then began to row with me. At first I tried too hard, plunging the oars deep into the water and using all my strength to bring them up again. But after a while, I figured out that if I loosened up and let the oar skim the water, the river would work with me instead of against me.

The little town was just as busy and vibrant as it had been when we drove through it on my first day in Santa Sofia. Zac stopped and chatted with almost everyone we passed. I didn't mind, though—it gave me time to look around. The shops were small and tidy. Inside the grocery store, I looked at the colorful packages of food that lined each aisle, trying to guess what was in each one. Although I had learned to say a handful of words in Portuguese, I still couldn't read it.

After Zac paid for the groceries, he continued chatting with the cashier for a while longer. It was clear how much my brother was liked here in Santa Sofia. He seemed at home.

As we walked out of the market, I hooked my brother's arm in mine. "When are you coming back?" I asked.

"We'll head back in a few minutes," Zac said. "I just need to find a few more of the items on Olivia's grocery list."

"No, I meant when are you coming back to St. Louis?" I said.

"Oh. Well, you know I've got another half a year in Brazil," he said, picking up a pineapple from the fruit stand. "I'm going to see if maybe I can extend my studies and stay here a little longer, though. There's word that a new group of poachers has moved into this area. If there's any way I can help stop them, I'd like to try."

I hesitated. "But you *are* coming home, right? I mean, you're not staying in Brazil forever, are you?"

Zac put down the basket. He knit his brow and shook his head. "Lea," he said, "I'm lucky enough to have discovered my passion. I want

A Gift

to help save the Amazon rainforest, and the best place to do that would be here in Brazil."

I felt a lump in my throat. I didn't know what to say.

My brother continued. "I have to be honest with you: My studies and my work are going to take me all over the world. I'm not sure how often I'll be able to come home. But even though we may be far apart, I'll always be your brother. I'll always be thinking of you."

I remained quiet as I gathered my thoughts, and then I looked up at him with a smile. "Maybe I can visit you all over the world!" I said.

Zac grinned. "I'd love that." He gave me a hug and I hugged him back twice as hard.

"What did you buy?" Olivia asked when we got back to the house.

"Everything on your list," I said, double-checking. "Papayas, rice, beans—"

"Oh, I meant for yourself," she said. "I thought you were going to buy some souvenirs."

I put my hand on my purse. I had forgotten about shopping for myself.

I had just logged on to my laptop when I heard Zac call out, "Lea, Marcos is back and said we can use the truck now. Let's you and Tomás and I go visit Amanda!"

I only had time to glance at an e-mail that Camila had sent, saying that her mother said she could visit me during my spring break—and that was only about six weeks away! Although I was already starting to feel sad about leaving Zac and Amanda tomorrow, my heart lifted at the thought of seeing Camila again.

As we drove past the dense green wall of trees that bordered the road, I felt glad that I had spring break to look forward to. Camila had been so great taking me around Praia Tropical, and I couldn't wait to return the favor and show her St. Louis. Plus, she was going to get to meet Abby and, of course, Ginger. I just wished she could have met Amanda.

Up ahead, I saw some bushes with bright pink flowers. "Zac, look," I said. "Hibiscus!"

"For Amanda," Tomás said, knowing what
I was thinking.

Zac pulled over and we all got out.

"Olha!" Tomás said. The hibiscus bush was
abuzz with a flock of rainbow-colored hummingbirds. We watched in awe as the tiny birds zipped
from flower to flower, dipping their long beaks
into the center of each bloom.

Tomás picked hibiscus flowers for Amanda
while I took a few photos of the hummingbirds.
Then we hopped back into the truck, as excited as
ever to see our adorable little friend.

At last, Zac drove up the gravel driveway
that led to the wildlife sanctuary. The truck
had barely stopped before I unbuckled my seat
belt and ran inside. Tomás and Zac were close
behind.

"Amanda? Erika?" I called out. I raced to
Amanda's bed. It was empty, except for Macaco.
"Amanda," I said softly. Where was she? And then
I had a terrible thought: *Am I too late? Did she—*

"Lea!" said someone behind me. It was Erika,
and she was holding Amanda.

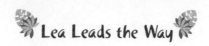

"Oh, thank goodness!" I said. "How's she doing today?"

"I've just weighed her, and—well, the antibiotics aren't battling the infection quite as well as we had hoped."

"Is she going to be okay?" I asked, steeling myself for bad news.

"We're doing the best we can," Erika said.

I noticed that she hadn't answered my question.

My voice quivered when I asked, "May I hold her?"

Erika nodded. "Of course. She'd like that."

I handed my camera to Tomás as I brought Amanda close to me. Her bath from the day before had worked wonders. Amanda's fur was still soft and she smelled great as I snuggled her. I never wanted to let her go.

"What will happen to her if—I mean *when* she gets better?" I asked as I held out the hibiscus flower and she began to nibble on it.

"If this little one can recover from her injuries and infection," Erika said, "she'll likely stay

here for a while. After all, Amanda is still a baby.
The missing claws may be a problem, but we'll
try to train her to latch on to trees without them.
When she's ready, we'll reintroduce her to the
rainforest. If she doesn't take to the forest, or if
her missing claws prove to be a problem, we'll
find a safe place for her. She'll either stay here or,
possibly, at a wildlife preserve. But for now, let's
just see whether she can recover."

I hugged Amanda again and whispered,
"You can do it. I know you can!"

The Flow of the River
Chapter 15

That night, I stayed up late to write my final blog post from Brazil. I looked around for my camera to download the latest photos—but I couldn't find it. For a moment I panicked, until I remembered that I had probably left it in the truck. It was too dark for me to go outside on my own to retrieve the camera, so I made a mental note to grab it from the truck before our sunrise cruise the next morning. Luckily, I had plenty of other photos already loaded on my tablet. I lingered over the photos of Amanda. Just thinking about her made my heart happy and sad at the same time.

I touched my wrist, expecting to find my pink wish bracelet—but it was gone! That's when I realized that it had granted me not just one wish—that Camila and I would always be great friends—but two more friendships that I hadn't expected.

I started typing my last post from the rainforest:

At first I thought that Amanda was lucky I found her when I did, but the more I think about it, the more I realize that I'm the one who was lucky. Amanda has helped me see that the rainforest is not just a place on a map, but a home for millions of animals who need our help. One way we can help is to raise awareness of the dangers that face this unique environment, which is home to so many amazing animals.

Now that I have traveled from the coast of Brazil to deep in the Amazon rainforest, I love this country and everything in it. I hope that someday I can return. Until then, I'm leaving a piece of my heart behind.

I didn't know exactly when or where my wish bracelet had fallen off, but I did know that it was

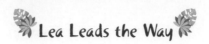
somewhere in the Amazon rainforest. I dedicated my last blog post to my three Brazilian friends: Camila, Tomás, and Amanda.

It seemed like I had just fallen asleep when it was time to wake up. It was still dark outside. I got dressed quickly, and then turned on my tablet to see if any of my classmates had commented since last night.

Zac rushed past the door and then screeched to a halt. He looked around the room. "Lea, are you packed yet? You're leaving today, so if we're going to get out on the river to watch the sunrise, you need to be packed before we go."

I threw my tablet on the bed and began stuffing my pajamas into my suitcase. Zac picked up my tablet and started scrolling through my blog.

I looked up. "My class has learned a lot about the rainforest," I told him. "Me too."

Zac nodded. "I can see that. I knew you took great photos, but the way you've written about the rainforest and Amanda is very moving. I'll bet if more people were able to read your blog, it would help bring some attention to what's going on here with deforestation and poaching."

"You really think so?" I asked.

He nodded.

My heart fluttered. If Zac liked what I had been posting, then maybe others would as well. Even though I'd be back in St. Louis all too soon, the rainforest and its wildlife would still be in danger and its story would need to be told. Zac could help me with that, and Erika and Marcos and Olivia, and even Tomás. *Especially* Tomás. Like me and my classmates, he was a part of the next generation—so what we did or did not do could determine the future of the rainforest.

I closed my suitcase and turned back to my tablet. At the bottom of last night's post, I added,

To be continued …

Tomás and Olivia were still asleep, but Zac was right behind me as we climbed into the canoe with Marcos. It was pitch black except for the light of the moon. As the canoe glided across the glassy black water, the buzz of cicadas and the croaking of tree frogs filled the air. Animals were all around me. They always had been.

"Get ready for one of the most incredible sights you'll ever see," Zac said.

I reached into my bag for my camera. *Oh no!* I had forgotten that it was still in Marcos's truck.

We rounded a bend and then glided down the river to where it opened up for miles and land was far away. There, Marcos cut the motor and let the canoe drift silently.

A warm pink-and-orange glow on the horizon reflected in the water as the sun began to rise. For a moment the sun hid behind some clouds, lighting them up from within. As the sun rose higher, the white clouds spread across the great expanse of sky that was now turning a light blue. Without the camera lens in front of me, I had a panoramic view of the river. Instead of taking a photo, I felt as though I were part of one. It was the most beautiful sight I had ever seen. I took

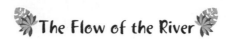

a mental picture, and knew it was something
I would never forget.

When we returned, Tomás was waiting
outside with my camera in his hands. I'd forgotten that I had handed it to him yesterday when
I held Amanda. He must have had it this whole
time.

"Obrigada," I said, ruffling his hair.

Tomás followed me inside and into the
bedroom, and sat next to my open suitcase with a
frown. He looked up at me with tears in his eyes.

"I know," I said. "I'll miss you, too."

I turned around to grab my sweatshirt off
the back of the desk chair, and when I turned
back, Tomás was gone.

"Lea!" Zac called out. "Time to go."

I closed my suitcase and grabbed my backpack, making sure that Ama's travel journal
was in there. I planned to finish reading it on
the plane. I also double-checked to make sure
I had my camera this time.

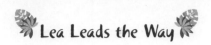

I thought I had put my flip-flops by the bedroom door, but they were gone. I searched Tomás's room, looking under the bed, in the closet, and behind the door. They were nowhere to be found, so I dug a pair of sneakers out of my bag instead. I said one last good-bye to the Barroses' house and headed out the door.

Olivia hugged me tight as we stood next to the truck. "Come back anytime," she said. "We love your brother and we love you, Lea."

Marcos joined in for a group hug. "It has been wonderful getting to meet Zac's sister," he said. "Although now I'll think of him as Lea's brother," he joked.

"Where's Tomás?" I asked, eyeing Galo Louco, who was glaring at me from the edge of the yard. When he came near, I tossed a piece of apple that I had saved from breakfast at his feet. He clucked happily as he ate his treat.

Olivia shook her head. "I think Tomás is hiding," she said. "He was very sad this morning."

I felt a tug on my heart. "I can't leave without saying good-bye to him."

"Lea, we really should leave now if we're going to stop and see Amanda before we head to the airport," Zac said.

"Give me a minute," I told him. "I think I know where he is."

I went to the big tree where Tomás had given me the palm-leaf crown. "Tomás?" I said. "Tomás, I know you're up there." The leaves rustled. "Tomás, I want to say good-bye." One of my flip-flops dropped to the ground, followed by the other one. I couldn't help smiling. Tomás must have thought that if I didn't have my shoes, I'd have to stay!

"Tomás, I have to go now," I said.

The leaves rustled again and he climbed down slowly. I gave him a huge hug. When he started to cry, I bent down and wiped the tears from his face. He reached into his pocket and handed me a folded piece of paper. I opened it and smiled. It was a drawing of Amanda, him, and me. I held it to my heart and thanked him.

"You are like a brother to me," I told him. "Brother. *Irmão.*"

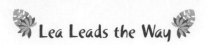

This made him smile. He pointed to me and said, "*Irmã*. Sister."

"So what do you think of your first international adventure?" Zac asked as he drove. "You swam in the ocean—and even in the Amazon River!—you created a wonderful blog about Brazil, and you rescued a baby sloth!"

I smiled. "And I made friends with a crazy chicken," I added. "Don't forget that!"

We both broke out laughing. I thought about the Meeting of the Waters at the beginning of my visit to the rainforest, where the river flowed black on one side and light coffee brown on the other. Maybe that was like Zac and me. We were very different and we always would be. But like the river, we were side by side, moving in the same direction, giving each other strength—and together we could really accomplish something. After all, together we had helped rescue Dad when he fell off the cliff, we had rescued and found a home for Amanda, and now we would

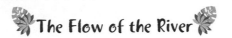

help spread the word of the dangers that faced the rainforest. I couldn't have done any of those things alone, nor would I have wanted to.

A Legacy
Chapter 16

My heart beat faster the closer we got to the wildlife sanctuary. I needed to know how Amanda was doing. A plan was beginning to take shape in my mind, but it sort of depended on Amanda.

I pulled out Ama's travel journal and thumbed through it until I found the pages I was looking for: the story about Georgie, the young giraffe my grandmother had adopted in Tanzania.

Zac had called Erika and let her know we were coming, and she and Amanda met us outside. Something had changed in Amanda. Her eyes sparkled as she raised her paw up to play with Erika's dangling earring.

"Someone had a great night," Erika said, laughing. "The medication finally kicked in. That

happens sometimes, because we're not always sure what dosage or what prescriptions will work best for each animal."

"So she's going to survive?" I asked hopefully.

"It looks like it," Erika said, grinning. Without my having to ask, she placed Amanda in my arms. "This little girl has a lot of spunk for a sloth!"

"I know someone else who could sometimes be mistaken for a sloth, but has a lot of spunk," Zac teased, nudging me.

I ignored him. "Erika," I said as I held the baby sloth close, "I'd like to adopt her."

"Lea, we've been through this," Zac said, lowering his voice. "You can't take her home with you."

"That's not what I meant. I want to help pay for her food or medication, or whatever she needs," I said. "I have some money from my birthday that I've saved, and I'm going to set aside some of my allowance every week. Plus, I'm pretty sure I can get some other kids at school to contribute, too. I'm hoping that with your help,

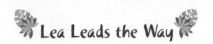
I can follow Amanda's journey on my blog. Maybe you could keep me updated?"

"I would gladly do that, Lea." Erika smiled. "And we would be happy to accept your donation. You could be Amanda's fairy godmother!"

I grinned and kissed the baby sloth. "Even though I may be far away," I whispered to her, "I will always be thinking of you."

It was a tearful farewell as Mom and Dad embraced Zac, and more crying when I said good-bye to him. But I knew that we would be connected through my blog—and that some-day I'd get to visit him in exotic places all over the world.

As the plane took off, I looked out the window. The green Amazon rainforest went on for miles, but I knew now that the rainforest and its wildlife wouldn't go on forever unless we humans did more to preserve it.

I picked up my camera to take some aerial photos, and then I scrolled through the photos of

my trip. I smiled when I saw the shots of Tomás looking at the margays and made a mental note to send them to him. That's when I noticed that there were pictures on the camera I didn't remember taking. Most were blurry and oddly cropped, but a few were in focus. They were of me! There I was holding Amanda: There was one shot of us nose-to-nose, another with Amanda's head on my shoulder, and yet another of us looking lovingly at each other.

Who took these photos? I wondered. Slowly it dawned on me: Tomás. He'd had my camera for my last twenty-four hours in Brazil, and he'd been using it.

"Thank you, Tomás," I whispered. I had always been so busy behind the camera that there were few photos of me in front of it.

I put the camera down and settled in with Ama's last travel journal. I was eager to read about more of her adventures. She had just visited Egypt and was looking forward to seeing Beijing. But when I turned the page, it was blank. I turned another page, and then another—they were all

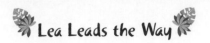

blank. I turned back to her last entry, and that's when it hit me. The date was around the same time Ama had learned she was sick. She never did make it to Beijing.

My heart felt heavy as I looked out the window at Brazil below me. I wished there was some way I could keep Ama's legacy alive. Then I had an idea. I scrounged around my backpack for a pen, and I opened Ama's journal to the first blank page. I took a deep breath, and wrote:

My name is Lea Clark, and I am Amanda Cooper's granddaughter. Like Ama, I am an adventurer. Recently, I visited Brazil, where I met a new friend, found a little brother, and became the fairy godmother for a baby sloth named Amanda.

Glossary of Portuguese Words

NOTE: In the pronunciation guide below, you'll sometimes see a small *m* or *n* at the end of a syllable. In these places, pronounce the letter very gently or don't quite finish saying it. In Brazil, an *l* at the end of a word is often pronounced "oo."

Amazonas *(ah-mah-ZOH-nahss)*—Amazon

bem-vinda *(beh^m VEE^n-dah)*—welcome (spoken to females)

bom dia *(boh^m JEE-ah)*—good morning

Bom trabalho. *(boh^m trah-BAHL-yo)*—Good job.

boto *(BOH-toh)*—a pink freshwater dolphin

Brilha, brilha, estrelinha . . . *(BREEL-yah BREEL-yah ehs-tray-LEEN-yah)*—Twinkle, twinkle, little star

carambola *(cah-rahm-BOH-lah)*—a tropical fruit shaped like a star

de nada *(juh NAH-dah)*—you're welcome

Está aí? *(ess-TAH ah-EE)*—Are you there?

Esta é a minha irmã. *(EHSS-tah eh ah MEE^n-yuh eer-MAH^n)*—This is my sister.

Galo Louco *(GAH-loh LOH-oo-coh)*—crazy rooster

irmã *(eer-MAH^n)*—sister

irmão *(eer-MAHW)*—brother

macaco *(mah-CAH-coo)*—monkey

mãe *(maee)*—mother

meu *(MAY-oo)*—my or mine

moqueca *(mo-KEH-kuh)*—a Brazilian seafood stew made with coconut milk, red palm oil, tomatoes, onions, garlic, and coriander

muito prazer *(moo-EE-too prah-ZEHR)*—much pleasure; an expression used when you first meet someone

Não estou aqui. *(NAH-oo ess-TOH ah-KEE)*—I'm not here.

obrigada *(o-bree-GAH-duh)*—thank you (spoken by females)

obrigado *(o-bree-GAH-doo)*—thank you (spoken by males)

oi *(oy)*—hi

olá *(o-LAH)*—hello

Olha! *(OHL-yah)*—Look!

Onde você está? *(OH^n-day voh-SAY ess-TAH)*—Where are you?

O que? *(oh KAY)*—What?

pão de queijo *(pahw deh KAY-ho)*—cheesy bread rolls

Por que você está chorando? *(pohr kay voh-SAY ess-TAH sho-RAH^n-doh)*—Why are you crying?

praia *(PRAH-yuh)*—beach

saboroso *(sah-boh-ROH-soh)*—very tasty

vem *(veh^m)*—come

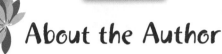

About the Author

Lisa Yee has written over a dozen books for young people. She loves to research and was thrilled when Lea's stories took her to the Bahia coast of Brazil. There, she snorkeled among the coral reefs, sampled local foods, and learned about the traditions and customs of the region. Lisa also visited the Amazon rainforest, where she fished for piranhas, swam in the Amazon River, and even ate roasted larvae during a hike. However, the highlights of her travels were meeting a caiman, a boa constrictor, and a baby sloth—though not all at once!

You can learn more about Lisa at www.lisayee.com and see photos of her Brazilian adventures.